THE HIRONO CHRONICLES

WOLF WARRIORS

THOMAS JOHN HOWARD BOGGIS

FIRST PRINTING, December 2020.
Harry Markos, Director.

Paperback: ISBN 978-1-913802-16-5
eBook: ISBN 978-1-913802-17-2

Book design by: Ian Sharman

Cover art and world map by: Mark Gerrard

Editor: Stephen Davis

www.markosia.com

First Edition

THE HIRONO CHRONICLES SERIES

BOOK ONE:
MEERA

BOOK TWO:
WOLF WARRIORS

AND COMING SOON:

BOOK THREE:
SPIRIT WAR

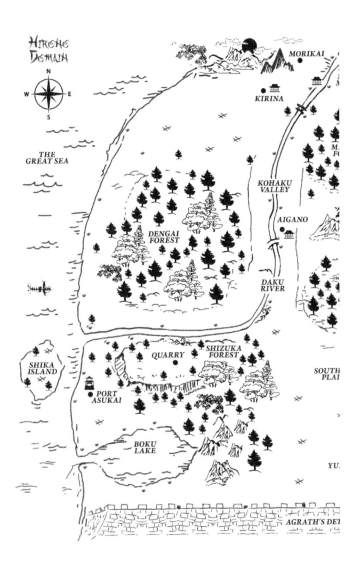

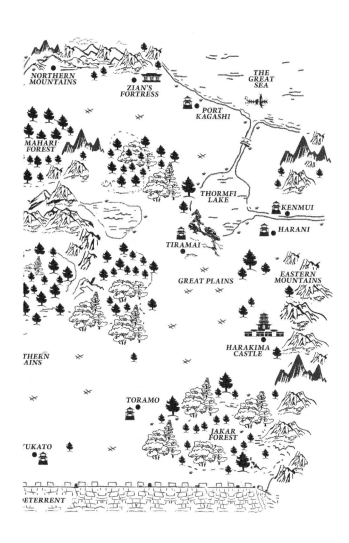

PROLOGUE

Her piercing amber gaze bored into him, reflecting back a part of himself he was only beginning to understand. Like her, he sensed things all around him - the smell of damp earth and burning wood, the sounds of a nearby stream, the wind in the treetops - but his focus remained entirely on those eyes. He felt that something had changed; something was different but he could not put his finger on it. There was something she wanted him to know, but her feelings were confused and difficult to understand, or perhaps what she wanted to tell him was merely difficult to say.

She had to go away. He had deciphered that much from her feelings, but why and where she was going remained a mystery to him. He had felt it himself. The inexorable force that gripped her tighter every day, calling her away to some place to which he could not yet follow her.

But he did not want her to go, not so soon after he had found her again. He felt adrift and it was only her spirit that anchored him down. Without her, he would float aimlessly, ever awaiting her return.

Her eyes betrayed the inescapable nature of the force acting upon her and she broke eye contact and looked westwards through the trees to where the source of this power clearly emanated. Her muscles tensed and it was clear she had to leave. He wanted to stop her but he knew that what she had to do was of great importance. How he knew, he could not explain, for she would not speak of it to him. She looked again into his face.

'Do not worry,' she said, and he understood this not through words exactly, but somehow through the feelings he could now sense. *'We will meet again soon; one way or another, we will run away together my love.'*

There was a flash of grey fur and she was gone, disappearing off west between the trees.

He stood up then, knowing it was time to move on. He could feel a nagging force pulling at himself now and it was leading him back; back to a place he never thought he would return to. But he knew he must go there, for something grave was happening in the east and he would have to offer whatever help he could...

CHAPTER ONE

I had been running for many weeks. Ever since I left Harakima castle, running from place to place; running for so long that sometimes I forgot what it was I was running from to begin with. For as long as I was running, I was also searching; searching for her, and when at last I found her, I felt I no longer had to run anymore. When I was with Meera everything was different. I slept better than I had for many years, my insomnia all but gone. I had not known sleep like this since I was very young. But, of course, it was not the same as it had been when we had known each other at Harakima.

Since the moment I was reunited with her, she had been distant; constantly distracted by some force or destiny that sought to pull her away from me. It seemed difficult for her to focus on the here and now and her emotions were tangled up and difficult to read.

When she left me, after the force became too strong for her to ignore any longer, I was lost. I felt certain that something important and frightening was happening in the east and that I must return to

Harakima, a place I never wanted to see again. But all I really wanted to do was resume running, and maybe one day, if it was meant to be, I would find her once more.

After she left, my sleeping became more and more disturbed. I would wake often during the night and find myself unable to go back to sleep, and when I did sleep all I dreamt about was her, but every night she seemed further away from me.

I did not know what to do. So, I simply began walking and let my feet take me where they would. For days I wandered and at last it became clear where I was being led, and I could fight it no longer. If Harakima was where I was meant to be, then that is where I would go.

For many days I continued my slow walk northward through the Jakar Forest to Harakima, hampered slightly by a limp – the result of a nasty wound I had sustained, what felt like decades ago. I had all but run out of the good food given to me by the people of the castle town and my pack – which contained many rolls of parchment detailing the events surrounding Orran's Blade – felt like a lead weight. My eyelids were once again heavy with sleep and the duel swords that hung at my side almost dragged me to the ground as my insomnia worsened daily.

While I may have been groggy and aching with tiredness, I was surprised to notice that most of my senses were as sharp and attuned as ever; maybe even more so. I heard the sound of a bird alighting on a maple tree fifty paces in front of me. I smelt a deer moving softly through the fallen leaves a great distance to my left – I smelt its fear and its desire to return to the herd. I was confused; how was I able to discern these things? It was strange indeed, but I reasoned with myself that the wind must have carried these sounds and smells in my direction - I could think of no other explanation.

The sound of footsteps approaching through the leaf mould, north of my current position, roused me from my thoughts. During the weeks alone after I left Harakima, I had encountered several groups of thieves and bandits and invariably would be forced to kill or injure them as they attempted to steal from me. Several days ago, during one of my infrequent bouts of troubled sleep, I had been taken by surprise by two elderly thieves, who were only looking for a crust of bread to keep them going another day or two. Startled out of my troubled dreams, I leapt up and through bleary eyes mistook the club one of them held for a sword. I reacted and cut him down before I had even had chance to dash the sleep from my eyes. The other thief dropped the concealed dagger he held and gave me a watery-eyed look of fear and desperation before hobbling off as quickly as his aged bones would allow.

It was these such experiences that made me wary of other humans wandering the forest. A slight metallic scrape was the only sound I made as I drew a sword from its scabbard and settled myself behind a screen of leaves in a hollow at the base of a tree. From here I could clearly see a figure tramping slowly through the trees in my direction. My eyes opened wide in shock and surprise as I recognised the man striding obliviously towards me. It couldn't be! What on earth would he be doing here?

He carried what looked like a near empty food pack. His hair was longer than I remembered it and he looked dishevelled, as though he had been travelling for many days, but it was undeniably him. The last thing I heard was that he had been dismissed – perhaps his life had gone to pieces and he had taken up as a bandit...?

'Shjin?' I asked uncertainly, standing up from my hiding place and letting my blade hang loosely at my side. I had expected my appearance to startle him, but instead he simply looked relieved. With a quick wave Shjin Kitano walked briskly towards me.

'Takashi,' Shjin said with a grateful smile as he took my hand and shook it firmly. 'Oh... I'm sorry; I heard you no longer go by that name. I was told to call you simply, Wolf.'

I nodded in reply. I did not know where to begin. So much had happened since we had last seen each other. The mere sight of him brought back memories of the events at Zian's fortress; the battle with the dragon Aralano, the discovery of the true root of my insomnia and of course... her death.

'What are you doing here?' I asked finally. 'Did Lord Orran dismiss you? I haven't seen you since...' I trailed off. Shjin sighed deeply and passed a hand through his bedraggled hair.

'Ahh, there is much I wish to tell you of my own affairs, but there are more important things to be discussed first.' He put an arm around my shoulders and started walking me in a northerly direction towards Harakima. 'You have been sent for by Lord Orran; he has had men out looking for you for over a week. You are a difficult man to track down,' he added with a rakish smile.

'Why... what does Lord Orran wish to speak to me about?' I asked. I was confused at this strange turn of events, but I suppose I could not deny that I had felt the first stirrings of something big on the horizon. Whatever Lord Orran wished to tell me, I knew with certainty it would not be good news.

Shjin lowered his voice when next he spoke, as though he believed we were being followed.

'There is a rumour flying around Harakima that... that you can converse with wolves.' Whatever I had expected to be told, this was not how I had expected it to begin.

It was during the battle at Zian's fortress, shortly after she was killed, that I first truly felt this deeply-embedded side of me taking hold, slowly awakening and gradually strengthening within me. Kamari later told me that, after seeing her fall, I had looked more like a wolf than a man.

I still did not profess to understand this side of myself, but I felt it growing daily and with it came a stark feeling of inevitability that I could not begin to guess at the origins of. My ability to converse with her grew steadily after we were reunited, but I had somehow always known that not even this boundary could stand between us.

I had no idea how this rumour could have started, but what I did know was that Lord Orran had spies everywhere. It was possible that, at some point over the last few weeks, someone had seen me with her and carried the information back to him.

'I suppose… I suppose I can, yes,' I began slowly. 'I can speak with her, with Meera, but I have not tried speaking to any other wolves.'

'Meera?' Shjin asked in confusion. Then a look of dawning comprehension crossed his face and he looked at me with an almost fatherly smile. 'So, you found her again, did you?' he said, staring intensely into my face. 'I knew from the beginning that nothing would stop you being together. Where is she now?'

'She had to leave…' I said after a very long pause. Almost overcome by emotion, I looked away, making it clear I did not want to discuss it further.

'So, for once one of the rumours in Harakima is true,' said Shjin, changing the course of the conversation.

'Why does this… ability interest Lord Orran?' I asked.

'Lord Orran wishes to discuss that with you himself, but what I will say is that time is not on our side and things are becoming desperate.'

Shjin tensed suddenly at a slight noise away to his right and his hand flew to his sword. The inquisitive bird that had made the noise fluttered off in fright and Shjin relaxed.

'You wanted to know what I have been up to since last we met,' Shjin said calmly, gradually speeding up our march northwards.

In the days following the defeat of Zian at his fortress, Shjin's life had been turned upside down and his reputation almost irreparably tarnished. The news had travelled fast around Harakima that it had been Shjin who stole Orran's Blade and delivered it into Zian's hands, but what was less well known was that he had only done it because Zian was holding prisoner and torturing Shjin's secret family.

Lord Orran had been sympathetic to Shjin's story and I knew it had been terribly hard upon Shjin to confess everything, including revealing the wife he had taken in secret behind his lord's back. Given the degree of his crimes and the general feeling within Harakima – even though his motives were understandable – Lord Orran had had no choice but to dismiss Shjin and allow him to return to his family in Harani village.

All of this had taken place before I woke up in Harakima after the battle at Zian's fortress. Since

then, Shjin had been living peacefully with his
family in Harani, communicating with Lord Orran
by messenger. His family had been greatly shaken
by their terrifying ordeal and it took many days for
them to fully recover from the shock. But at last,
Shjin finally felt happy. His secret was out and he no
longer had to carry the burden of shame of hiding it
from his lord. The time spent with his children was
no longer covert and stolen, and for many days he
was happier than he had ever been.

After what had happened, Shjin was
understandably protective of his family, and so
when he received a letter from Lord Orran ordering
him to evacuate the village and bring both his family
and the other villagers back to Harakima, he did not
waste a second.

'Why did Lord Orran order the evacuation?' I
asked, frowning. 'What is going on in the east that
worries him so?'

Shjin looked at me in surprise.

'What makes you think something is happening
in the east?'

'I'm not sure,' I answered truthfully. 'But I suppose I
sensed something big was happening through Meera.'

'Well, as I said, Lord Orran will fill you in when
you arrive,' Shjin said. 'Anyway, when I reached
Harakima with the entire population of Harani
behind me, I was met by Lord Orran and he asked if
I would not mind leaving straight away to find you.'
Shjin paused here and looked off in the direction of

Harakima, as though he could see his family even from this distance. 'He gave me a pack of food and sent me on my way, telling me my family would be well looked after and far safer in Harakima than in Harani. I did not see how I could refuse,' he concluded with a small smile.

'Well, I'm glad it was you that found me,' I answered, glancing up at him.

The final stretch of the journey took us a few days on empty stomachs, travelling through heavy rain and driving winds. When at last we came within sight of Harakima, I was afforded the ominous view of the darkened castle against a grey-black bank of storm clouds. Thunder roared in the distance and I knew at once that this was the work of the spirits, demonstrating their anger at whatever was brewing in the east. If the spirits were angry, then it must be something terrible, and evil.

As we splashed through deepening puddles in the grass, I looked up at the wall-tops where so much had taken place. On those walls I had killed men, and seen comrades fall. I recalled vividly the deaths of two new friends at Harakima, Hitoshi and Yohji; and I remembered the effect their deaths had had on our friend, Katsu.

I remembered the night I met Meera on the walls and realised she loved me, only to make the crippling discovery that she was in an arranged marriage to Shjin. I stopped suddenly as an overwhelming urge to run away gripped me. What was I doing back here? This place held nothing but bad memories for me and I had half turned before Shjin put a comforting hand on my shoulder.

'Don't worry,' he said encouragingly. 'It will be alright, trust me.'

It was only his steadying spirit that prevented me from fleeing there and then. Slowly, we began walking again and as I looked up, I noticed the sky had begun to lighten as the storm clouds gradually passed over Harakima and into the east.

The long walk from the first tier of the castle to the third was a difficult experience and one I will not forget in a hurry. Wherever I walked, people turned to stare at me, villagers and Kurai alike, and I felt myself shrink under their unblinking eyes. Being back here was almost more than I could bear. In the second tier we passed the very spot where Meera's body had been burned on a pyre, along with a paper effigy of a wolf to aid her spirit's journey. I clutched the pendant at my throat that bore the likeness of a female wolf; the pendant that had once belonged to Meera. I missed her so much.

As we walked, I noticed that many of the villagers and Kurai were staring at Shjin, anger and hatred in their eyes, and I remembered that they did not know the full story regarding his theft of Orran's Blade. It was not only me who found it hard to return here.

By the time we reached the third tier where the castle stood, I could feel myself shaking under the pressure of so many emotions. For a time at least, Lord Orran had held me responsible for the death of Meera, his daughter. When I left Harakima he had stopped me to apologise and explain that he did not really blame me, but I wondered whether he had truly meant what he said. I had often thought myself that it might have been better if I had never come to Harakima, or had died in the first battle outside its walls.

With surety of purpose, Shjin led me towards the castle along the narrow sunken path that was bordered by chest-high stone walls. It looked just as I remembered it, but then I realised it had only been a matter of months since I had last been here. To me it felt like a lifetime ago. The same fat carp still swam serenely in the ornamental fish pond, unfazed by the goings-on around them. The cherry trees were as I remembered them, except that they were no longer in bloom. We walked along the path that skirted the pond and approached the tall, many-tiered castle that reached high into the grey sky above us.

A retainer slid open the door to admit us on hands and knees, casting a sly, furious look at Shjin before moving aside to admit us into the main hall. I entered slowly and glanced quickly around. The first thing I noticed was by far the most obvious, worrying and saddening. After the battle at Zian's fortress, there were very few Kurai left to continue in the service of their lord. Where there had once been two columns of five Kurai warriors facing each other across the room, there were now only three men left, each sitting in the exact places I remembered. Upon seeing this grave and disheartening sight, I recalled that I had not seen many Kurai on the wall-tops either. Lord Orran's army was indeed severely depleted.

As was customary when given an audience with a lord, I kept my eyes averted from him and bowed formally to the floor, kneeling on a straw mat placed there for the purpose. The stone floor felt ice cold as I touched my head to it and remained prostrate, awaiting the invitation to sit up. Orran considered me for what felt like an age before bidding me to look at him.

During the time I spent at Harakima, I had watched Lord Orran change from a strong, powerful man – who exuded strength and confidence – to an empty husk of his former self, as anger and worry crippled him, seeming to age him by many years. Today I was seeing him at his lowest ebb. If I did not know better, I would believe I was looking at a different man entirely. His index finger and thumb were massaging the bridge of his crooked nose and there were blue-black bags under his eyes, as though he too had not slept for many days. His unkempt hair was now almost completely grey and his beard was much longer than usual.

'You are an exceedingly difficult man to track down… Wolf,' he said at last. I almost smiled at hearing the same words Shjin had spoken when we met, but I managed to keep my face in check.

'I am sorry I have caused you so much trouble my lord,' I replied, bowing my head briefly to the floor once more, 'but I never wanted to be found by anyone.' Orran studied me from his seated position at the top of a small flight of stairs, but did not say anything. 'Shjin told me you have something urgent you wish to speak to me about?' I continued uncertainly.

'Urgent?' Orran said at last. 'Urgent is not the word for it, we are far beyond urgent.' Orran put his fingertips together and looked at me over the top of them. 'We are fast running out of time and you are one of our last remaining… realistic hopes.' He stood and began pacing up and down, his hands clasped behind his back. 'No doubt you have heard tell of one of the Orrans' greatest enemies through the generations, the Kichibei Clan?'

I nodded. I knew the story well. Hirono had once been divided into many smaller provinces and the first Lord Kichibei had ruled several of them. For a time, the individual lords had been happy controlling their own separate provinces, but it was a state of affairs that was never going to last long. A fierce battle for control ensued and after many gruelling years, it was the Orran line that eventually drove out or destroyed the other lords and unified the provinces into what was now known as the Hirono Domain.

'Well, ever since Kichibei lost control of his provinces in Hirono, he, and his descendants, have been living out their years on a small archipelago of islands off the eastern coast of our land,' Orran began, still pacing. 'Their current lord, a man named Shigako Kichibei, has made an attempt to retake Hirono before, but we swiftly put him down. However, my spies tell me that he has once more amassed a large following and now commands a vast army. All these years since they were driven from Hirono, they have been waiting for their opportunity to retake this land, a land they believe is rightfully theirs. They have already failed once, but after learning of the battle at Zian's fortress... they have finally seen their golden opportunity.'

Even though I had sensed something bad on the horizon, I had not imagined a threat on this scale; a very real threat that could spell the end of the Orran bloodline and the Kurai.

'Kichibei and his army would never have been a match for the full strength of the Kurai, but that did not stop him last time – not even the threat of Aralano was enough to deter him...' Orran said as he stopped pacing and slumped back into a sitting position. 'Now, with Aralano gone and my Kurai all but dead, the only advantage we have over Kichibei are the walls that surround Harakima. We have sent out messengers to every domain we are friendly with but have had no responses and do not expect any. We have but one final option, one last fleeting chance of salvation. It is said that you can speak with wolves...'

I had been waiting for this and was not quite sure how to answer.

'What do you wish of me, my lord?' I said at last.

'You know of the legends that surround the passing of a Kurai warrior from this world to the next,' he began. It was not a question. He knew why I left Harakima – he knew who I was searching for and I could tell he wanted to discuss it, but there was no time… He continued anyway. 'After death, a strong Kurai warrior's spirit will not leave this earth. Instead, they are reborn in the skin of a wolf so that they may remain a guardian of this land and of the Kurai. Down through the generations the wolves have always been there to aid us whenever we needed them, but until now they have always known when we required help. For some reason we have had neither sight nor sound of any wolves for years, since well before the battle at Zian's fortress. We need you… Wolf… to head out into the west – where they are rumoured to hold council – find the wolves, and persuade them to come to Harakima's aid once again.'

I had already foreseen this eventuality, but still almost fell over in shock.

My head was reeling from the weight of the task that had been dropped on my shoulders. I was barely able to take anything in as I was hurried from the main hall and taken down to the first tier of the castle by Shjin. I found it hard to comprehend the magnitude of the job I had been given, but I was certain that this path I had been started on was the correct, no… the *only* path I could walk.

I stood by Shjin near the main gate, shaking slightly as a laden horse was led over to us by a stable boy. He bowed to us and I detected a desperate light shining in his eyes. Clearly the news of impending attack was not a secret.

I looked at the horse and realised with surprise and delight that it was Dagri, the horse that had been with me through many of my previous adventures. He was somewhat shy and jumpy by nature, but he was the finest example of his kind I had ever seen.

'Dagri!' I said happily, stroking the horse's neck. 'I lost him several weeks ago when I was attacked by bandits - how did he get back here?' I asked Shjin.

'I did not witness it personally, but I believe he just turned up one day,' Shjin replied, his eyes fixed on the horse. 'He did the same after the battle at Zian's fortress, must have known he would be needed here…'

As Shjin helped me into Dagri's saddle I noticed that the villagers nearby were still looking at Shjin with anger and resentment.

'Are you going to be alright?' I asked him, looking at the surrounding villagers, only realising then how silly those words sounded coming from my mouth.

'I'm going to be fine,' Shjin said, but he could not hide his anxiety. 'I will explain everything to the people of Harakima when you leave, it's you I'm worried about. It would be best if you could recruit someone to go with you on your journey. I would of course accompany you, but Lord Orran wishes me to stay here and I do not want to disobey him.'

'I have an idea who to take with me,' I said, with a smile I could barely keep in place. Shjin gave me another of his fatherly looks as he arranged the packs of food more securely on Dagri's back.

'You are very brave,' he said, raising his head to meet my eyes. 'I know I will see you return very soon.'

With that he waved at the guards to open the gate and slapped the horse's flank. Dagri whinnied and broke into a canter, carrying me out of the gates and across the flats in front of the castle town.

Lord Orran had told me that the wolves held council somewhere near the coast, in the far west, and so I set my sights in that direction. But before I went there, I had a small but necessary detour to make…

CHAPTER TWO

The wind ruffled my hair as Dagri settled into an easy pace, the packs of food thumping gently against his muscular flanks. The cool air was welcome and refreshing, helping to clear my head and keep at bay the sleep that once again threatened to overwhelm me.

As I rode – instead of thinking about the hardships that lay ahead – I thought about the last time I had travelled this same route. It had been when I had made the journey to Harakima for the first time. Back then I had been accompanied by my best friend Kamari Shiro and we had not had horses to speed us on our way. But there were still some similarities. Just like last time I was battling with insomnia, I was afraid and confused by the events taking place around me and, as last time, I was filled with an inexplicable sense of inevitability – pulling me along like a current, guiding my way and my decisions – that led me to believe that everything that was happening was happening for a reason.

The sky above was beginning to darken; tendrils of dark blue were punching their way through the dreary grey and casting long shadows across the land.

I had already covered a great distance and knew that it would be best to find a place to spend the night so Dagri could get some rest. I remembered a place nearby we had stopped at during the first journey to Harakima and veered slightly north to reach it, my ears pricked.

It was not long before I heard what I was listening for. A small stream cut southwards through the landscape and I turned Dagri towards the sound of water gurgling over submerged rocks. I allowed Dagri to drink at the night-dark water before tethering him to a nearby tree where he knelt down and began to happily chew grass. I filled a small cup from the ice-cold stream and drank deeply before settling down with my back against a tree near Dagri. I knew I should have some food to keep my strength up, but I also knew that I simply could not force myself to eat anything right now. I felt a lump the size of an apple in my throat, as I thought about everything that lay ahead of me. Returning to Aigano was going to be difficult, almost as difficult as returning to Harakima had been.

When I think of Aigano, one memory always springs to the fore, a memory that will haunt me for the rest of my days. I remember standing in a paralysed state of shock and fear, watching helplessly as my father was cut down by three foreign mercenaries on the bridge at the centre of the village. I remember watching his blood spread slowly across the wooden boards and drip soundlessly into the fast-flowing river below. I often wonder what would have happened if I had intervened – if I had fought his attackers instead of standing there like a statue, if I had only…

I thrust the memory swiftly and unceremoniously from my thoughts, for this was the only way I would be able to return at all – if I simply forced myself not to think about it. I knew that if I started to dwell on the "what ifs", I would quickly lose myself to madness. I unrolled my sleeping mat at the base of the tree and lay down, determined to try and get a little sleep. I shut my eyes, and tried to blank my mind.

I sat up suddenly but could not explain what had caused it, for I was sure it was not a sound that had roused me. I had the strange feeling that I might not be awake at all, but everything seemed so real. Some instinct told me I was not alone, but as I scanned the area around me, I could detect nothing obvious. It was only when I strained my eyes that I discerned a shape on the opposite bank in the darkness between the trees. It was a familiar shape, but it was not human…

The shadowy form of a wolf regarded me from across the stream. Its ears were pricked forwards as though I was speaking and it was listening, but there was not a sound to be heard anywhere. I had the oddest feeling that I recognised this wolf. I sat up slowly but the wolf did not move a muscle.

'Is that… is that you?' I asked incredulously, my voice sounding croaky to my ears. The wolf did not make a sound as I stood up and began to walk towards it. Still believing that I might be asleep, I rubbed my eyes, but by the time I looked back, the wolf had gone – vanished – as though it had been made of nothing more than black smoke. I crawled back to my mat and lay down, filled with a bizarre feeling that I could not even begin to explain.

When I awoke in the morning, I still did not know for certain whether the vision of the wolf had occurred in reality or in the realm of sleep. Instead of brooding on this, I quickly built up a fire and set some water from the stream to boil. Taking a handful of dry rice from the pack on Dagri's back, I dropped them into the bubbling water and sat back to watch it boil. I thought of nothing while the rice cooked and simply stared at the spot where the wolf, or whatever it might have been, had appeared to me last night.

When the rice was ready, I ate it plain, with nothing to sweeten it. I washed out my bowl and drank some water before dousing the fire and packing everything I had used back onto Dagri. I clambered into Dagri's saddle and set off westwards again towards Aigano.

The sun hung low in the sky behind me, shining weakly out of a cloud-strewn, grey sky as Kohaku Valley drew ever closer. The prospect of seeing my mother and sister and Kamari again made me eager to reach Aigano swiftly, but still the memories of that night repelled me from my home town. Do not think about it, I kept telling myself, do not think about it…

It was early afternoon by the time I reached the southern end of Kohaku Valley. A strong southerly breeze had begun to blow as though ushering me away from Aigano, but I carried on regardless, following the river that split the valley from north to south. The familiar smells, sights and sounds awakened many fond memories from my childhood, and some that I was less fond of… Even at this distance, I could smell the oxen and wood smoke from the village, I could hear the comforting sounds of the Daku River, and the first truly familiar sight was the shrine to the Valley Spirit which had stood in a state of disrepair last time I had seen it. However, things had changed in the time since I had left.

Many of the slaves freed from Zian's fortress had returned with my family, Kamari, his wife Ellia – now officially a Kurai warrior – and the other Aigano inhabitants, to rebuild the village and settle there as an outpost of Harakima, and by the look of things they had been very busy indeed.

I was delighted to see that the shrine to the Valley Spirit was in the process of being restored to its former magnificence. Soon the villagers would once again be able to pray there for good harvests and a peaceful year. But what pleased me most of all was seeing all the new houses that had been built, extending the village almost to the point it had been in the old days.

Our pace had slowed considerably; after pushing Dagri so hard to get here I found that all I wanted to do was put off the moment of my return as long as possible. I slid from the saddle and allowed Dagri to drink from the river, deciding to lead the horse the rest of the way.

When I finally entered the main area of the village, it was a rather unusual experience. Just as in Harakima, all of the villagers turned to stare at me, but as I passed, they bowed down low to the floor, murmuring their thanks. In their faces I saw the light of renewed respect glowing like starlight and it made me feel glad, despite myself. I smiled at the thought of how much Kamari must be enjoying this reborn respect for our families. I remembered his fierce resentment towards the villagers for not showing the Asano and Shiro families the proper esteem, but that was only until the battle at Zian's fortress, when Kamari finally realised that respect is earned and not given freely.

By the time I reached the ornate, crimson-painted bridge that spanned the Daku River, the whispering had broken out all around me, sounding for all the world like a strong wind through the treetops. The last time I had been here and walked this path through the village, the atmosphere had been very different indeed. The looks directed at me and the tone of the whispers had been angry and malicious, and I had felt fear, sadness, and even anger - though not as strong as Kamari's.

I stopped on the bridge – forcing myself not to dwell on what had happened here – and turned full-circle, taking in my surroundings. The village was situated in a steep-sided valley, the slopes of which were dotted with maple and cedar trees. My family's house was built on the western bank of the river, part way up the slope, with Kamari's house further north along the valley, and higher-up the slope. The main bulk of the now greatly extended village was built on the eastern bank of the river, along with the shrine, training grounds, rice paddies and animal pens.

I looked back at my house. My home. It felt like years since I had last seen or spoken to Kamari and my family, and I was unsure what I would say to them first. I did not have long to wait, however. Looking over at Kamari's house, I spotted him emerging into the daylight through the sliding front door. He was rubbing his eyes sleepily and it was not until he had stretched mightily that he noticed me standing stock-still on the bridge. I smiled at the look of shock and pleasure on his face as he stumbled down the wooden steps outside his house and hurried towards me as fast as his sleep-heavy limbs would allow.

'Just woken up, have you?' I said, with as best a laugh as I could manage. 'I've been riding for hours already.'

Kamari seemed unable to say anything and simply enveloped me in a bone-bending hug. He seemed even stronger than I remembered him; clearly, his renewed importance had motivated him to mould himself into what he imagined was essential in a leader of men. I was a mere stick insect in comparison to him.

'Takash... Wolf,' Kamari began, holding me at arm's length and looking into my face. 'We were beginning to wonder if you were ever coming back!'

I looked into his eyes then and saw something – or perhaps sensed something – that I did not understand. Some hidden emotion seemed to be struggling against his relieved and happy exterior – fighting to get out – but I had no idea what it could be and couldn't think how to broach it. I put it to the back of my mind and resolved to ask him about it later. Whatever it was, it could wait – I had more pressing things to deal with. Or so I thought...

'I've had a lot to think about, I needed... time,' I answered, looking past Kamari towards my house.

'What's wrong?' said Kamari, looking more closely into my face and taking a step back. 'There's something going on, isn't there?'

'There is indeed my friend, but this is something that concerns everyone. I will discuss it with my mother, you and Ellia first, before we tell the rest of the village; then I have a favour to ask of you...'

Kamari looked both worried and confused at this, but simply nodded his head and led the way to my house, from which issued the aroma of freshly prepared herbal tea. I took off my sandals when we reached the front door and Kamari slid it open and passed inside. I took a deep breath and, after a few seconds, followed him in.

The inside of the house was at once familiar and alienating. As I walked across the wooden floorboards, I recalled exactly which ones creaked and which didn't, a knowledge picked up from my many sleepless nights wandering the house. At first glance, everything seemed the same as I remembered it and a well-known and well-loved childhood sense of security began to settle into my chest. However, there were many differences that I only noticed upon closer inspection. I remembered then that the house had been damaged when the foreign mercenaries attacked, so bits had been rebuilt or redecorated here and there, but clearly, my mother had taken great pains for the house to look exactly as it had before the attack.

Kamari slid open the door to the main room of the house and tried hard to suppress the smile that was spreading across his face.

'Look who finally decided to come home!' he said cheerfully. I stepped into view and took in the occupants of the room in which, for many years, I had sat and eaten breakfast. My mother was seated cross-legged on a straw mat by the low table. Kneeling at her side was Ellia, who was handing her a steaming cup of herbal tea. At the sound of Kamari's voice, they both looked up and saw me. My mother appeared pale; whether this was due to the shock of seeing me or something else, I did not know, but when she looked at me, I saw the relief and pleasure in her face and realised – with a wrench of guilt – that she had been wondering whether she would ever see me again. A huge smile had broken out on Ellia's face at the sight of me. For a time, no one said anything and we all simply looked at each other. It was my mother who finally broke the silence. She looked as though she had been going to stand up, but then thought better of it and instead held out her arms to me. I walked across the room and knelt down beside her and she hugged me fiercely, as though unwilling to ever let go.

'Takashi,' she mumbled, her voice thick with unshed tears. 'It's so good to see you.'

'He is known as Wolf now,' Kamari said quietly from across the room.

'I respect your feelings on everything that happened,' she said to me. 'But you are my son – my Takashi – and that is who will you will always be to me.'

We drew apart and sat looking at each other.

'As much as I want to believe that you came here just to see us,' my mother continued, 'I can see there are other reasons too.' I smiled at how well she knew me.

'I have been looking forward to seeing you all again ever since I left Harakima,' I said truthfully. 'But you're right. Hirono and the Kurai are in terrible danger and I was sent into the west by Lord Orran to find aid.'

I then explained to them everything I had been told by Lord Orran, detailing the threat from Lord

Kichibei, the seriously diminished numbers of the Kurai, and my desperate task to bring the wolves to Harakima's aid. Ellia in particular seemed shocked and appalled by this news. She of course had lived her entire life in Harakima and thus knew all about the history of the feud with the Kichibei clan; she in fact knew a great deal more about the situation than I did.

'We had long anticipated something like this,' Ellia said, her voice low and furious. 'But even now I know it is happening, I find it hard to comprehend Kichibei's cowardice and lack of honour, to attack us in our crippled state.'

She was livid with anger, but I think this masked the fear she was feeling for her brethren in the Kurai and the people of Hirono. I glanced over at Kamari and saw that he looked pale and worried, but I could also tell that he had discerned why I had made the detour to Aigano, when time was of the essence. He already knew what I would ask of him...

'You wish me to go with you,' he said, almost to himself. It was not a question.

I was unsure what to say to this. I had never really contemplated not doing this with him. Now I stopped to think about it, I realised that I was in fact asking an awful lot of him. I was asking him to risk his life when he had only recently been married to the woman he loves. He had other commitments now and so when he took risks, he had to think, not just about himself, but his wife too. I could never forgive myself if Ellia was left a widow due to me asking a favour of my friend. But this was not just some vain personal quest. I was asking him to help prevent an outcome that would impact every man, woman and child in Hirono. I knew him well enough to know that, had he not been married, he would have agreed without a moment's hesitation.

'I will not be able to do this without you,' I said looking straight into his eyes.

'Wolf, there is something I have not yet told you,' Kamari answered slowly. 'I am going to be a father.'

CHAPTER THREE

At first, I was too surprised and pleased for them to think of anything to say in response. I could hardly believe I had not noticed it sooner, and so for a few moments I simply sat in stunned silence.

'That is wonderful news, I am so happy for you both!' I said at last, breaking out in a wide smile. 'I had no idea at all!'

Of course, this news changed everything. How could I possibly ask Kamari to come with me now? If, spirits forbid, something were to happen to him on our journey, then he would be leaving behind not only a loving wife but a child as well, who would grow up without a father's guiding hand.

Again, I could see that Kamari knew exactly what I was thinking. I could see the light of pride for his new family shining in his face, but so too could I see the excitement at the prospect of another adventure burning within him. I did not know what to do. Surely, I could not allow him to come with me? I could not put this choice before him…

'Kamari, I…'

'Of course, I'm still going with you,' Kamari cut across me, the ghost of a smile flitting across his face.

'But... but this is going to be dangerous... think about your wife... your unborn child...'

'They are forever in my thoughts, and that is why I will go with you,' he replied.

'Kamari, I don't...'

'If I don't help you and you were to fail in your task,' Kamari said, interrupting me again, 'then the land we know and love could be overrun, and my child may never be born at all.'

I looked from Kamari to Ellia and back again. My mother watched the proceedings in silence and I could see pride in her face too.

'Ellia will agree with me on this,' Kamari continued when I said nothing.

'Of course,' Ellia said. 'I would expect nothing less from my husband. I would go with you myself if I were not pregnant.'

For a moment I dithered, cursing myself for ever coming here to ask this of my friend, then I nodded in acquiescence. I could see the truth in everything he said, hear the conviction in his voice, and to be honest, I could not stem the feeling of relief that washed over me at the knowledge that my best friend would be coming with me on my journey.

'Thank you, brother,' I said quietly, bowing my head to him.

'Now, we must inform and organise the villagers,' Kamari said, the leader in him stepping forth and taking command. 'They cannot stay here.'

'No, they cannot of course,' I said in agreement. 'The safest place for them right now is within the walls of Harakima. Is it likely that when Kichibei's army arrives, he will send out skirmish parties to comb Hirono; it is too dangerous for them to stay here.'

'If time is as short as you say, then we have not a moment to waste,' said Kamari. 'We must call a meeting of the villagers at once.'

It was late afternoon by the time the entire population of Aigano had assembled in the centre of the village. It was a blustery day and the wind that blew between the wooden houses was strong. It set everyone's clothes dancing and whipped the dust into miniature whirlwinds to sting eyes and bite at arms and hands. Young children huddled close to their mothers and everywhere I looked, eyes were narrowed against the vicious wind.

Kamari, Ellia and I stood on a raised platform before the bemused and whispering villagers. My mother had opted to stay in the house, having heard the news already. To tell the truth, I was a bit worried about her. Ever since I had arrived back in Aigano, she had been acting a little oddly. It was possibly something to do with my sudden return, but perhaps it ran deeper; maybe the root of her behaviour was more to do with the changes that had occurred in me since last we met…

Kamari called for quiet, but his voice was whipped away in the howling wind and most of the villagers were not even aware he had spoken. But Kamari was unperturbed. When he next spoke, his voice carried a force and authority I had rarely heard there before.

'Quiet, please!'

At once, a hush fell over the gathering as every head turned towards us. I felt extremely nervous under the combined stares of all these people, but Kamari did not seem at all bothered. I realised then that ever since Kamari had returned to Aigano with the other villagers, he had been a figure of great authority. He will have organised, instructed and overseen all of the building and repair work done on the village, so he would by now be used to this.

'You are all of course wondering why I called this meeting in such unfavourable conditions,' Kamari said, in a voice that all could hear clearly. 'And you will all be wondering at the return of Wolf here,' Kamari said, gesturing at me and heightening my nerves, 'who most of you will have known as Takashi Asano.' Heads bobbed in agreement and eyes flicked between Kamari and me. 'These past few months we have been through a lot together. From the events at Zian Miyoshi's fortress to the rebuilding of our shattered village and lives, each of you has conducted them self admirably. It is this spirit of honour and community we have rebuilt that I hope – I know – will hold steady when I tell you that we now face another great and terrible threat, that will once more uproot us from our homes.'

Kamari then went on to explain everything I had related to him about Kichibei and his army, and his plans to retake Hirono and eradicate the Kurai. He went on to explain that I had been sent into the west to gather an army for Lord Orran. I was stunned at the power of his words – he really seemed to me to be a true leader of men – and I knew that he would make a superb warrior general.

As Kamari's speech drew near its end, the whispering broke out again and worried expressions spread through the crowd like wildfire, but to Kamari's obvious satisfaction, no one openly panicked.

'In the face of this approaching army, you must travel to the safest place in Hirono,' Kamari said, his voice once again quieting the villagers. 'All of you must leave Aigano as soon as humanly possible and travel south-east to Harakima, where Lord Orran will be expecting you. Travel light, do not overburden yourselves with personal treasures, and always stick together. Honour your family, and those in your community, as though they were your family.'

'You sound as though you will not be coming with us?' one of the villagers piped-up from the crowd. I recognised the speaker as Shio Takami, the son of Yaram Takami, who was killed while protecting my father from Zian's foreign mercenaries. He was about my age and looked strong and intelligent, and I could see at once what Kamari's next move would be.

'You are right Shio,' Kamari began carefully. 'I will not be accompanying you to Harakima, for I will be heading into the west with Wolf to gather an army for Lord Orran.' I noticed that Kamari had wisely decided to leave out the fact that we had been sent to gather an army of wolves and I was grateful to him for it, for this would raise far too many questions and I had neither the desire nor the time to answer them. 'In my absence, I appoint you, Shio, to lead your fellow villagers to Harakima – I believe you do know its exact location?'

'I do indeed, Kamari,' Shio said with a deep bow, a proud smile obvious on his face. 'Thank you.'

It was a mark of how strong the villagers' respect for Kamari had become that none of the older men in the village questioned this appointment.

'I would stay and help you organise everyone to leave,' Kamari continued, 'but Wolf and I have precious little time and must leave immediately. I trust that you will not dally and will leave as quickly as possible. And I trust that the rest of you will look to Shio as you would look to me,' Kamari said, indicating to the other Aigano villagers. 'Respect his decisions, follow his commands, and I hope that we will all be reunited soon.'

Together, Kamari, Ellia and I stepped down from the platform and passed through the silent crowd who parted before us, all eyes following our progress. I did not look around, but from behind, I heard Shio's voice fill the air, loud and confident.

'You all heard what Kamari said, we are about to leave our village again, but this time we do so on our own terms and of our own free will. This time we choose to leave because it is what is best for our families. Pack sparingly, gather enough food for a five-day journey, and make sure that the animals are secure in their pens, for we will be coming back, that I promise you.'

With these words alone, I knew that Kamari had made the right decision in choosing Shio to lead the villagers to Harakima.

Everything seemed to be happening so quickly that it was difficult to take it all in. It seemed like only minutes ago that I had met Shjin in the forest and been told that Lord Orran wanted to speak with me. And now here I was, about to pack up and leave Aigano again with Kamari by my side. But again, I felt pervaded by that same feeling of inevitability; like I was being swept down a river and could neither reach nor see the bank. With this in mind I tried to focus only on what I had to do and aimed to block out everything else.

We had just crossed the bridge on the way back to my home and already the village behind us was a hive of activity as the villagers prepared for the long journey to Harakima. It was a lot easier for the Aigano villagers to prepare for their journey – as they had an almost exact estimate of how long their journey would last – whereas Kamari and I had no idea how long it would take us to reach the western shore, where the wolves were believed to hold council.

Kamari and Ellia hurried off to their home to pack, telling me that they would meet me as soon as possible. Alone, I took off my sandals and stepped through the sliding door into my home. I heard voices and movement in the main room and so headed there first. My mother was seated in the same place I had last seen her and she was speaking earnestly to my little sister Mia. A flush of guilt gripped me as I realised that I had completely forgotten about her, in light of everything else going on. I felt ashamed that I had forgotten someone so dear to me. When she saw me, she rushed across the room and I knelt down to hug her tightly. I could feel her shaking and when we drew apart, I could see there were tears in her eyes.

'Takashi... you aren't going to leave already, are you?' she said in a quavering voice. I did not have the heart to correct her on my name. It felt like so long since I had last seen her that I too could barely keep my voice steady as I answered.

'I am afraid we will all have to leave here soon,' I replied, knowing that my answer would offer no comfort. 'But where you are going, I will not be able to follow just yet; I have something very important I must do before we will see each other again.'

'What is so important that it keeps you away from us?' she asked, the question catching me by surprise. It was only then that I realised how much she had grown and matured since I had last truly spent any time with her, well before the events at Zian's fortress. She was only eight summers old, but she had already seen and experienced so many things that children of her age should not even read about. Her bravery was astonishing, but I was not sure that she would understand me when I told her that I had no real choice in whether to leave or not.

'Trust me,' I began, looking into her face. 'I would not leave you again if it were not of vital importance.'

She did not say anything else, and after one last lingering look at me, she turned and disappeared through the doorway towards her room.

'She does not understand why you stayed away for so long,' my mother said into the fledgling silence, as though she had read my thoughts. 'And she cannot understand why you must leave us again.'

'I'm leaving because Hirono is under threat from Lord Kichibei's army,' I said uncertainly. 'Can she not understand that? Is that not what you were just speaking to her about?'

'It was,' my mother replied. 'But we both know there is more to your decision to leave again than just that.'

Those words stuck with me forever after, for my mother had fathomed the very feelings that in truth drove my every thought and deed. In the end, it all came back to her. For me, everything revolved around her...

It felt like returning to consciousness when Kamari and Ellia entered my house and came into the main room. Those few minutes since my mother had last spoken felt like days as we sat staring motionless at each other.

'Are you ready to go now, Wolf?' Kamari asked, sounding slightly unsure of himself. I understood his hesitation; it must have been a strange sight to walk in and see us sitting stock-still in complete silence.

'I am,' I said quickly, glancing at my mother before standing up. I had not unpacked the things I had brought from Harakima, so with the addition of some extra food for the journey, I was indeed ready to go.

'Then it is best if we make this quick and do not linger,' Kamari said, flicking his eyes between each of us. 'We have a long journey ahead of us.'

We packed as much food onto Dagri as he could comfortably bear and made ready to depart. Kamari followed me back into the house where my mother was still seated, so we could say our goodbyes. Ellia moved to stand next to Kamari as I knelt down by my mother's side and hugged her, kissing her on the forehead.

'Ellia will look after you and Mia on the way to Harakima,' I said, looking into her eyes. As I said this, I noticed a look pass between Kamari and Ellia out of the corner of my eye, but I did not understand its significance. 'I will meet you at Harakima,' I continued, kissing her on the cheek once more, 'and do not worry, Hirono will be safe and you will see Aigano again.'

My mother was silent for a time, as though deep in thought. Then she spoke.

'We each follow our own paths; our own instincts and beliefs,' she said. Then, after a pause, 'I know yours will lead you right.'

I did not fully comprehend the meaning of this, at least not at first, but before I could question her further, she and Ellia had shooed me out of the room. My last glimpse of my mother was of her rubbing her sleeve across moist eyes.

Outside, Mia was waiting. She hugged me tightly around the waist, her eyes streaming with tears.

'Come back to us safely,' she said, disappearing back inside the house before I had the chance to say goodbye to her.

Ellia walked Kamari and I towards Dagri, who was tethered near the western bank of the river. She stopped and wrapped her arms around her husband, kissing him passionately before releasing him, somewhat embarrassed in front of me.

'You know I would go with you if I could,' she said to Kamari with a slight smile.

'And I would be glad to have you with us,' Kamari said, returning the smile. 'I would feel safer each night,' he ended with a laugh. She mock punched her husband on the arm and stepped back a few paces, her eyes dry.

Leading Dagri by his reins, Kamari and I walked south along the western river bank, following the direction of the valley before we would be able to turn off south-west and begin the long march to the western shore.

CHAPTER FOUR

Our south-westerly course saw us crossing the river and entering Shizuka Forest shortly after exiting Kohaku Valley, the trees now pressing in around us like the bars of a cell. Dead leaves drifted serenely down from above to land in great heaps against the massed tree trunks.

We had been walking for quite some time before I finally decided to question him. I had thought a lot about my parting conversations in Aigano and there were some aspects of them that I had yet to understand.

'I get the impression there is something you are not telling me, Kamari,' I said at last, looking over at him. 'I noticed the look that passed between you and Ellia when I was saying goodbye to my mother.'

'You are imagining things, Wolf,' he answered, after a pause, 'it was simply an emotional moment for all of us, to say goodbye.'

I was not entirely sure, but I believe Kamari did not quite meet my eye as he said this. I decided not to press him any further, but I felt sure there was something there – something I would have to prise out of him eventually.

It was dark between the trees, the only illumination afforded by the occasional strand of sunlight that punched through the lofty canopy above. The atmosphere all around was close and oppressive. What little sound to be heard was indistinct and hushed, as though the birds and beasts were afraid to disturb the quiet. Mimicking the inhabitants of the forest, we walked in silence for some time, our minds focussed only on maintaining our south-westerly heading.

After about an hour or so, I decided to try and lighten the mood a little.

'So, you haven't yet told me what you've been up to since I left Harakima,' I said, in a voice barely above a whisper. I can't describe what it is, but something about quiet places always seems to warrant speaking in whispers. To me, this silent forest felt like the kind of place where spirits would reside and if that was the case, it would be best not to disturb them. 'I see you've been supervising the rebuilding of Aigano, but what else have you been doing?' I stumbled on an exposed tree root and Kamari steadied me with his left hand without breaking step.

'Well, you were at the wedding of course,' he began, staring wistfully off into the space between the trees. 'The one good thing to come out of everything that happened; if Zian had never come here with his mercenaries, I would not have met Ellia.' I smiled at him as he said this. It seemed clear to me that he and Ellia were meant to be together;

even if Zian had never come back to Hirono, I believe their paths would have crossed at some stage in their lives. 'Almost as soon as we were married, she told me she wanted children. I resisted at first – I needed time to think things through, get a plan for the future, but… you know how she is…' here he smiled proudly, 'and now we have one on the way.'

For a moment he was silent as he adjusted the pack on his back, then he continued.

'I might not have had a plan, but one thing I knew for certain was I wanted to move back home as soon as possible and the other Aigano villagers agreed, so we left only a few days after you did. Most of the other prisoners released from Zian's fortress needed new homes too, so they decided to come along with us. Organising that many people for the journey back to Aigano was difficult – I'm not going to lie – but we managed it without any major incidents. Once we were back, everything just became obvious, really… With so many more people we needed to build or rebuild homes, start planting crops, breed animals. And, well… after the battle at Zian's fortress, everyone just seemed to accept me as their leader, so it was my job to oversee the building work, and once everyone had a place to live, I called for the repair of the Valley Spirit's shrine. Other than that, well… I've simply been enjoying life with the woman I can no longer imagine being without.'

He glanced at me as we continued our steady pace through the trees with Dagri trotting quietly behind us. 'But throughout it all, you were in my thoughts. I could see the conviction in you when you left and I dearly hoped that you would find her, and this hope made me both pleased and worried...' I looked at him quizzically as he said this. 'It pleased me because I knew that finding her again meant everything to you, but I was worried that if you did find her, I would never see you again,' Kamari finished, dropping his eyes from my face and looking off into the trees.

'I did find her,' I said, my voice barely audible.

'Then... what happened to her?' Kamari asked in surprise.

'Something drew her away from me... something she believed she must do,' I answered.

'What?'

'I... I don't know yet,' I replied, my voice cracking slightly as I said it.

It was early evening but this deep in the forest it might as well have been midnight, for we could barely see our hands in front of our faces. We had slowed our pace and now walked with our arms held out in front of us like blind men. Even Kamari – who was always the one who wanted to push on hardest and longest – had to admit that we could go no further that day.

'If this is the time night falls in this forest, I hope we reach its end quickly,' Kamari growled in frustration.

We had stopped by the side of a fallen oak tree in the early stages of decay and decided that it would be the best place to spend the night, as it would afford at least some cover from both view and the elements. We also decided to risk a small fire, but the price of this was that we would have to take turns keeping watch during the night. I had of course been sleeping badly the past few weeks since Meera left, so I decided to take the first watch and simply not wake Kamari until morning. There was no point in both of us lying awake.

We cooked and ate a few of the mackerel we had brought, because if we did not eat them soon, they would simply go bad and attract animals. We accompanied the fish with bowls of rice and small glasses of heated rice wine to warm our insides. We gave some water to Dagri and tidied everything away, and Kamari agreed readily when I said I would go on first watch.

As usual, not even the discomfort of lying on a forest floor and the eeriness of our surroundings could prevent Kamari from falling asleep almost instantly. Within seconds of saying goodnight and making me promise to wake him after a few hours' sleep, his snores were already drifting up into the still air. I smiled at his inexplicable ability to sleep in any situation and sat with my back against the fallen oak tree, staring at a spot on the ground just in front of my feet. As usual during the long, sleepless night hours, my thoughts turned back to Meera and where she might be now. Some force had irresistibly called her and stolen her from me, and I could not help thinking – *what was so important that it kept her away from me?*

With a shock I realised that those were the exact words Mia had said to me in Aigano. I now understood her confusion and even her resentment. It was my feelings for her; my need for her, that had kept me away from my family, and now something was keeping her away from me…

I looked up. There had been no sound but some instinct told me to look up, and there it was again – the charcoal black form of a wolf standing between the trees, just on the edge of the firelight. It was closer than the last time I had seen it and I sensed something definitely familiar about it. Was I imagining this? Was this image triggered because I was thinking about her? Or was it something else? Something else entirely…

'Hey, Kamari,' I murmured, shaking him gently. Kamari grunted in his sleep and flapped his arm as though swatting a fly before turning onto his side and continuing to snore loudly. I looked back at where the wolf had stood only seconds before and was unsurprised to see it had again vanished, as though it could turn invisible at will.

I slumped back against the tree. What did it all mean? There were too many things going on at the moment that I did not understand and it did not help that I had barely slept in the past week. The familiar black and purple rings had reappeared around my eyes and my sight was blurred and unsteady. The chance to simply rest should be enough to keep me going tomorrow…

'Hey!' Kamari said, upon waking up next morning. 'You didn't wake me for my watch last night!'

'I did!' I replied tiredly, trying to suppress the smile that was threatening to betray me. 'I woke you up after a couple of hours and you took over, then you woke me to keep watch for the last few hours.'

'Did I?' Kamari asked, completely unsure of himself. 'I don't remember any of that…'

'You were probably half asleep, you know what you're like,' I answered, the smile now creeping across my face. Luckily, Kamari did not seem to notice as he was rolling up his sleeping mat and strolling over to check on Dagri. I had not bothered to unroll my own mat, so I picked up the tightly rolled bundle and began to tidy our campsite. Kamari stamped out the still glowing embers of the campfire and within minutes we were ready to go.

Kamari stepped forth with renewed vigour after enjoying an inexplicably good night's sleep. It was inexplicable because when he rolled up his mat, I saw that he had spent the entire night on what looked like a small boulder, which he apparently had not noticed. This was a side of him that would forever remain a mystery to me.

With Kamari marching ahead as though pursued by dragon fire, I was destined as ever to lag tiredly behind, enduring in good humour his many jokes about how slow I was. When he likened me to a tortoise, I forced my weary body to speed up and for a time I managed to keep pace with him. But my body had not known as much training as Kamari's, and so it was not long before I took up my position once more at the rear.

At about midday it began to rain, lightly at first, but growing heavier and heavier with every passing minute. As the rain came down, so too did my spirits. The rain even seemed to have dampened Kamari's mood, for he had ceased his light-hearted banter and joking. Huge droplets of rain were soon hammering down onto the tightly meshed canopy above, filtering through to fall to earth, churning the dirt and leaves into thick mud. My hair had grown unchecked for many months and the rain had matted it into a soaking curtain which, try as I might, I could not sweep out of my eyes.

Kamari had dropped back to tend to Dagri, who was nervous and slipping on the muddy ground. The sound of the rain was steadily growing in volume, incessantly drumming on the foliage above, only to pass through and smack the surfaces of the innumerable puddles that had sprung up everywhere.

'We need to find shelter!' I shouted above the noise of the rain and wind. Kamari simply nodded; his head bowed against the elements as he led Dagri along.

I do not know where they came from. They appeared so suddenly that when I looked up and discerned them through a watery haze, I stumbled in shock. Six men were ranged in a wide semi-circle between the trees ahead of us. Each of them stood perfectly still, their weapons drawn and held ready at their sides. Their eyes were fixed unblinkingly upon us and from them I sensed a hunger and menace that chilled me to my core.

Kamari had not noticed the men ahead. Still walking with his head bowed, he bumped into the back of me. This time I jumped in shock, believing there were more of them sneaking up behind us. I whirled around, drawing my sword at the same time.

'Don't just stand there,' Kamari said, raising his dripping head to look at me. 'We need to find...' He trailed off as his eyes took in my tense body and drawn weapon. 'What's the matter? Why have you...' His voice cut-off abruptly as he noticed the armed men blocking our way. I whipped around.

They were closer now. Their semi-circular formation was the same, but they were now a mere handful of paces in front of us. They remained standing stock-still and stared at us, that frightening feeling of hunger emanating from them stronger than ever.

It began so quickly as to almost defy belief. From a standing start, the man furthest to the right had begun running and bulled into me before I even had chance to raise my weapon. Kamari released his hold on Dagri's reins and the horse immediately bolted, cantering back down the path we had walked and coming to a stop at what he clearly believed was a safe distance. Kamari drew his sword and turned to meet his attackers.

The first man's attack had sent me sprawling in the mud where I slid and cracked my head against the base of a cedar. Almost without stopping, the man leapt into the air with a snarl, his blade held point-down, seeking to drive it through my belly and into the deep mud. Groggily, I just managed to roll to one side, but still felt the bite of his blade as it grazed my hip.

Still lying in the mud, my head feeling like it was splitting in two, I watched as the man made a second leap at me, swinging his blade wildly. I managed to deflect the haphazard blow, steel ringing on steel, and rolled away, hearing rather than seeing him slip and hit the mud beside me. With the man lying face down at my side, struggling to stand up in the slippery mud, I sat up swiftly and drove my blade downwards through his spine. Pinned to the ground, the man could do nothing but flail wildly, his face a picture of agony as his scream turned to a gurgle. Within seconds his body lay still, his hands and feet twitching occasionally. I withdrew my blade from his corpse and stood up quickly. I had a fleeting glimpse of Kamari – one man lying dead at his feet, two more clashing blades with him – before a figure obscured my vision, hurtling towards me with blade held high.

Anticipating where he would swing, I spun to my left and gripped his right arm as he passed, using his own momentum to send him head first into the trunk of a tree. As he staggered to his feet, I noticed that he was an elderly man. His ribs were clearly visible beneath his skin and, combined with his hollow cheeks, they gave him the appearance of a walking skeleton.

His legs were visibly wobbling beneath him as he came at me a second time, desperation lending him the strength to batter me backwards with his blade. I stumbled on the leg of the first man I had killed but still managed to parry the blows that were raining down. My attacker's right leg was now shaking severely and I saw my chance. Feinting to his right so that he would put all his weight on his weaker leg, I ducked back to my right and brought my blade up and across his throat, spinning away from him to face any further attackers. In this brief interlude I looked over at Kamari. He had cut down the second of his attackers, but seemed to be having trouble with the third. In fact, they were now engaged in a violent tug of war over Kamari's backpack, slashing at each other one-handed with their blades.

It became obvious why they were attacking us. They were simply starving bandits, much like the others who had sought to steal my food over the past few months. But these men seemed much more desperate; their souls were in shreds and now their single occupation in life was the search for food.

I had taken but one step towards them when the bandit managed to slash Kamari's hand open to the bone, forcing him to release his grip on the backpack. Kamari roared with pain as the bandit took to his heels and fled westwards through the trees. Gritting his teeth, Kamari forced himself into a run and sped-off in pursuit.

'Kamari! Kamari! Let it go!' I yelled after him. 'Just let it…'

But at that moment the sixth bandit, who I had almost forgotten about, threw down his sword and leapt onto my back with a yell that did not sound human. He latched onto my own backpack and tried to claw it from my shoulders. I tottered around, the man's weight bringing me to my knees. His grunts and snarls were almost feral as his fist thudded again and again into the side of my head while his free hand ripped one strap of the backpack. I was close to blacking-out when I managed to bring my elbow crunching full into the man's face. He yelled terrifyingly, blood spraying the back of my neck, as my elbow connected over and over with his nose and mouth.

He let go at last and fell to the ground, one hand clutching his face, the other clawing madly at the hilt of the blade he had dropped in his frenzied attempt to steal my pack. He hauled himself to his feet, but it was clear that he was not destined to stay in the vertical plain for long. His skinny, naked chest was bathed in crimson and his eyes appeared unfocussed and severely bloodshot.

Blood was thumping painfully in my temples and I swayed slightly as I rushed him, knocking aside his feeble defence and driving my sword through his chest. He slid off the blade and crumpled to the floor, his body instantly limp, his pain now over.

I sheathed my sword and clasped both my hands to my head – the pain was almost unbearable. I sank down at the base of a tree and drew my knees up under my chin, still clutching my head and feeling blood run between my fingers. Whether it was my blood or my attacker's, I could not tell.

'Kamari!' I yelled, hearing my voice break. 'Kamari! Where are you?'

CHAPTER FIVE

I lurched to my feet but a pain-induced wave of nausea swept through me and I fell back into the mud and vomited, setting my head pounding, fit to burst. I needed to pursue Kamari before he got too far but, in this state, I could barely stand, let alone track someone.

With one hand still holding my throbbing head, I groped inside my backpack and pulled out a flask of water and sipped from it for several minutes. The rain had died down a little but I was already covered in mud and soaked to the skin, and the chill wind that blew between the trees made me shiver.

As soon as I felt the pain subside, I got to my feet and again was consumed by nausea, but this time I kept my feet. I picked up my torn pack and walked unsteadily westwards after Kamari. Footprints and broken twigs in the mud showed the path he and his quarry had taken and so I followed this trail as it zigzagged through the trees.

I could not understand what had possessed Kamari to chase after the bandit like this. I knew what he could be like when his blood was up, but

I did not think he would risk losing me in the forest simply to finish the fight. For all he knew the bandit could have been leading him to more of his comrades to finish the job they had started.

A noise behind made me whirl around, but it was only Dagri trotting nervously towards me, his ears flicking in all directions, listening for any sound of attack. I walked slowly towards him, holding out my hands reassuringly. On reaching him I checked that none of the bags were missing and made sure they were still strapped tightly to his back. I stroked his nose and whispered words of encouragement as I began to lead him along Kamari's trail.

A faint, growling rumble could be heard, growing louder and louder the further west I went.

What is that? I thought. *Could it be thunder?*

I looked up but could not see the sky through the leaves above. It certainly sounded like thunder, but something about it seemed wrong… An ominous feeling descended upon me and I began to pick my way more carefully along Kamari's trail. It was then that I heard his yells, ringing out above the ever-increasing sound.

'Kamari!' I yelled, as I broke into a run, dragging the startled Dagri behind me. Branches whipped my face and arms as I ran and my head began to pound worse than ever; it was so bad that I could barely see and narrowly avoided blundering into trees.

Whatever the sound was it could not be thunder, for it was coming from somewhere directly ahead of me. With leaves and branches flashing by on either side, I sprinted towards the source of the noise, heedless of danger.

As I drew closer and closer, the pitch of the noise changed dramatically, becoming lower and more ferocious, carrying with it a palpable feeling of menace. At that moment I was jerked back by my hold on Dagri's reins. The horse had dug his hooves in and brought himself to a complete stop, yanking me off my feet. I sprawled in the mud once again, yelping at a spike of pain in my head as my neck whipped backwards.

Getting up swiftly, I made to continue on, but – try as I might – I could not force Dagri to move another step towards the source of the growling. He turned to face the east and tried to tug me in that direction. His intentions were clear; he would go no nearer that noise. I had no choice. I let go of the reins and continued on without him. Dagri turned to face me as I left, whinnying softly and stamping the ground, but he made no attempt to follow.

A burning sensation had begun to spread through my legs and I knew I would not be able to run much further, but Kamari's yells had stopped and I had begun to fear the worst. At last I broke through some bushes, my hands and face scratched and bleeding, and ran into the middle of a scene I will never forget. The first thing I took in was Kamari, standing so still he might have been carved from stone. His eyes were glassy and staring and his mouth hung slightly open. At his feet lay his sword, which had been dropped from nerveless hands. By his sword lay the body of the bandit he had been pursuing, whose blood still leaked into the muddy ground. It was several seconds, which felt like several minutes, before my mind was able to process the rest of this strange and terrifying scene.

Without knowing it – in my haste to reach Kamari – I had burst right into the middle of a ring of wolves. There must have been at least twenty of them, all grey wolves, but in my shocked and injured state I was not able to take an accurate count. Each of them was lean and powerfully built, their coats flecked with myriad shades of grey, white and black. They had been advancing slowly and threateningly towards Kamari – black lips drawn up in snarls, growls rumbling in every throat – but the second they saw me, their attitudes immediately changed. They did not back-off exactly, but nor did they advance any further. The snarls vanished from their lips but the growls persisted, changing in pitch and rhythm as though they were talking to each other. Their faces seemed to change too, taking on almost calculating expressions.

What happened next is difficult to explain, but I will try my best to describe it. It began as a kind of ringing in my ears – faintly at first – the sound weaving and melding with the wolf growls until it became one, single, unified note. And from this one note, recognisable sound patterns seemed to emerge. I would not call them words exactly; it was a complex mix of feelings and sounds that combined in my head to form something understandable. A language, I suppose you would call it, but it was unlike any I had ever encountered before or would ever encounter again.

In this tongue it was not possible to lie, for your feelings would always betray you – there was absolutely no falsity or double-speak, no hidden agendas or motives. In this tongue there was only simple, undeniable truth. It was the most beautiful language I had ever come across. In my normal language, emotions can be acted – you can fake a laugh even when you are sad, or utter angry words even if they are not truly meant and quickly regretted. But in this tongue they always knew. Anything you said would always be backed-up by your wholeheartedly truthful feelings. Nothing could be hidden. Everything was honest.

A male wolf stepped forward from the ring and looked at those around him. He was bigger and more powerful-looking than the other wolves hemming us in. An ugly scar ran down the left side of his head, just below the ear; the wound obvious as the hair had not grown back around it, leaving a bald patch. His ears swivelled this way and that and his mouth opened slightly, revealing many chipped but spear-sharp teeth.

'What are these humans doing in our forest?' the wolf communicated to those around him, mixed feelings of anger, menace and foreboding seeming to pulse from him. 'It is ominous indeed that they should appear at this time.'

Murmuring sprang up among the other wolves, heads flicked here and there and teeth were revealed in half snarls. I got the distinct impression that they knew what I was, but not why I was here, and I realised that if I did not explain myself quickly, things might turn nasty fast.

'We have been sent here to speak with the leader of the Council of Wolves,' I communicated hesitantly in wolf-speak, glancing at Kamari. Somehow, he managed to look even more shocked and stunned than ever before. I knew he would not be able to understand what I had just said, but I had no idea what it must sound like to his ears.

A ripple ran through the wolves immediately, as every head turned to look at the brother next to him. The wolf who had stepped forward cocked his head to one side and looked at me shrewdly.

'I sensed something about you,' the wolf said slowly, a distinct feeling of intrigue emanating from him. 'You speak our tongue.'

'That is why I was sent to speak to your Council leader,' I replied. 'It is a matter of extreme urgency.'

'What is your name?' the wolf asked.

'Wol... Takashi Asano,' I replied, deciding it would be better to give my birth name, rather than the name I had given myself.

'And your startled-looking friend?' he asked.

'His name is Kamari Shiro,' I answered, looking across at him. 'He came to help me find you.'

'Hmm,' the wolf said, staring at him too. 'He fights well enough, but clearly does not understand our tongue.'

For a few moments nothing was said as the huge wolf considered Kamari and I. At last he spoke.

'My name is Matai, I am second-in-command of the Council and responsible for the defence and protection of my brothers,' he said, taking a step closer. 'I will not allow you access to the Council unless you tell me why you wish to speak with us.'

I glanced around the massed wolves, feeling their eyes boring into me, their expressions ranging from mild anger to thoughtfulness. Then I took a deep breath and replied.

'A grave threat has been detected in the east and the situation at Harakima is dire,' I began. 'Lord Orran has sent us to make a request of your Council... a request for aid.'

At this, the voice of every wolf was raised in a cacophony of sound; some were angry, others resentful or disrespectful, others still called for quiet. Matai turned his head and snarled at his brothers until they lapsed into silence.

'I see,' Matai said once calm had been restored. 'Once again the Kurai are in need of our help. Is the Kurai spirit now so weak that they must call on us at the first hint of strife?'

I was not sure what to say to this, so instead I kept silent. I sensed that there was some disturbance in the wolf Council; some divide over the subject of Lord Orran and his Kurai, and I was about to walk right into the middle of it.

CHAPTER SIX

'If you are to accompany us back to the Council you must first relinquish your weapons to my brothers,' Matai said to Kamari and I as two wolves stepped towards us.

'They wish us to give them our swords,' I said to Kamari. He gave me a dubious glance but did not say anything. It was clear he had no intention of giving up his weapons.

'Why must we give you our weapons?' I asked, perplexed. 'Do you not trust us?'

'It is not a question of trust,' Matai answered. 'We know everything you have told us to be true.' There is no lying in this tongue I reminded myself. 'It is simply that weapons are not allowed to be openly displayed before the Council. It is a law,' he finished. I explained this to Kamari and he shook his head at me.

'How do we know they're telling the truth?' he asked worriedly. 'How do we know they won't attack as soon as we're defenceless?'

'Well, first of all, if they had wanted to attack us, they would have done so already, swords or no,' I began, looking at him seriously. 'And second, I *know* they are not lying to me. I cannot explain right now, so I ask you to just trust me and hand over your swords.'

Kamari was clearly unhappy about this, but at last handed over his swords wordlessly to the wolf that approached him. The wolf took the twin blades in his jaws and stood to one side. I gave my swords to the second wolf and Matai nodded in satisfaction.

'Follow me and we will lead you to the Council,' he said over his shoulder as he began to walk off westwards. I was about to follow when the wolves around us stiffened, turning their heads to look behind, their ears rigid and their noses taking in deep sniffs of the air. Two of the wolves broke-off and began to run back down the trail we had walked. I turned and spotted what it was they had seen. Dagri! The horse was following at a distance, frightened of the wolves, but unwilling to leave us behind. The wolves were closing on him and I knew he would not be able to outrun them in this dense forest.

'Wait!' I yelled in the wolf tongue. 'That horse belongs to us. He is carrying our belongings!'

Matai stopped still and howled. At once the two wolves, who had almost reached the terrified horse, abandoned their attack and hurried back to join us.

'Let us continue,' Matai said, as though nothing had happened.

I looked behind us and saw that Dagri had recovered from his shock already and was back on our trail, keeping as great a distance between him and the wolves as he could without losing sight of us.

With the wolves pressing closely around us as we walked – but more or less ignoring us – my attention turned instead to Kamari. His expression was troubled, thoughtful, and it made me wish that I could read minds, so I could hear exactly what he made of everything that had just happened. I got the impression that what he had witnessed had frightened him; or maybe it was not fright, but he had just seen a side of me he did not understand and I did not want it to become a barrier between us. We needed to talk about it. But I did not know what to say, how to even begin the conversation, and things were not helped by having the wolves all around us.

'That must have… that must have seemed pretty strange to you…' I eventually whispered lamely.

At first Kamari looked like he was struggling for a response. After what felt like minutes, I began wondering how else I could approach the subject, when at last he replied.

'I always knew there was something about you,' he said slowly, looking at the wolves walking purposefully around us. 'It's been there as long as I've known you, but I first truly saw it during the battle at Zian's fortress. Another part of you took over that day after Meera… after she… I tried not to think about it because I knew that however hard I tried, however long I spent, I would never fully comprehend it… and after seeing that today, I now know it for certain. I think this is a side of you that not even you will ever completely understand, but I also think – I *know* – that it is of great importance and its purpose and direction are only now beginning to be revealed to you… to us.'

So… Kamari could feel it too. This unsettling feeling of purpose, of an inevitable direction that surrounded me. But when would I discover what it meant and where it was leading me?

My throat was dry and so, with a little effort I asked, 'What did that language sound like to you?'

'Not if I was given a thousand years alone to think about it would I be able to describe what I heard,' he answered, his eyes still fixed on the wolves around us.

All of a sudden, I sensed movement in the trees to our right and at that moment I heard Matai growl a low command to the wolves around him:

'Kill them.'

The cold, emotionless way he said these two words sent a shiver down my spine as several wolves detached themselves from the main body and hurtled off between the trees. Within seconds, the quiet of the afternoon forest was shattered as screams and snarls rent the air, disturbing birds from their nests and sending them flapping and squawking indignantly into the air.

As the birds diminished to specks in the pale grey sky – their cries fading with them – the sounds of ripping and gurgling yells took their place once more. It was so horrific; I was on the verge of covering my ears when I spotted two emaciated men rushing blindly towards us through the trees.

Their thin bodies were criss-crossed with deep bites and scratches from which blood flowed freely. A huge grey wolf, his jaw smeared with bloody slaver, appeared from nowhere and pounced on the slower of the two men, knocking him almost out of sight behind a tree. All that could now be seen were the hind quarters of the wolf and the feet of the man, which were thrashing wildly beneath the considerable bulk of his attacker. The feet swiftly ceased their jerking and the wolf re-joined his brothers in pursuit of the last man, his jaws now dripping blood.

The last man continued to sprint towards us and our vanguard of wolves, as though unaware of our presence, but even at the speed he was running, he would not reach us before…

His legs buckled under the weight of the wolf that latched itself around his neck, carrying him to the floor. The wolf tore savagely at the back of his neck as the man tried to pull himself away on his stomach, his fingertips clawing the sodden earth. Somehow the man managed to throw a lucky elbow that caught the wolf directly in the left eye. The wolf leapt off him with a snarl of pain. Taking his chance, the man slipped and stumbled towards us, for all the world appearing to believe that we would offer him protection.

He had almost reached Kamari and I when the forerunner of the wolves caught him, knocking him to the floor once more and snapping at his throat. Up close, it was clear the man was a bandit and as he finally gave up the struggle – the life fading from his eyes – he seemed to notice me at last.

The scene that had just played out before me was terrible, horrifying, and may have left a scar on any other who witnessed it, but all I could think of at the time was – I was right. The bandit Kamari had chased, from whom to retrieve his pack, had indeed been leading him to more of his comrades.

'Those bandits are a blight on this land,' Matai said in explanation, making me jump in fright as I had not noticed him approach. 'They attack the weak and helpless and often work for our enemies, the men of the south. They are lost and hungry souls that have but one journey left to make.'

With that, he turned and stalked back to the head of the group, calling for us to begin marching again.

Throughout all this, Kamari's face had remained impassive. He had not been at all affected by the vicious deaths we had just witnessed. I had to ask him.

'Why did you chase after that bandit?' I asked suddenly, without preamble. 'He was leading you to those men,' I added, indicating the bodies behind us. 'You risked your own life and you risked losing me, and for what? To finish the fight? To retrieve a bit of food and an old pack?'

In answer, Kamari reached a hand into his pack and delved deeply. After several seconds he withdrew his hand, a small wooden object clasped tightly in it.

'What is that?' I asked in a hushed voice.

Kamari held it toward me so I could take a closer look. Depicted in polished maple wood were the unmistakeable figures of Kamari and Ellia, standing side by side, their arms wrapped around each other. Their expressions were so convincing, so believable, that it almost beggared belief – it was a moment captured in time. It was happiness untainted, joy and elation rolled into one.

'Who carved this?' I asked.

'It was Lord Orran,' Kamari answered, his eyes on the figurine but not seeming to really see it. 'He carved it on the day of our wedding and gave it to Ellia.'

'I didn't see him carving it,' I said, thinking back.

'Well, your mind was on other things,' Kamari replied. 'When it was finished, Orran gave it to Ellia and she gave it to me as a gift. I have treasured it ever since.'

He ran his fingers lovingly along the shiny surface of the wood before replacing it carefully in his backpack. I realised then why he had chased after the bandit so rashly in order to retrieve this carving. It was what the figurine stood for, more than the thing itself, that made it so important. It symbolised his wife – the being he most cherished on this earth – and he could not stand to see her in the hands of an evil man. His actions were infused with a rashness born of a soul-destroying fear for his wife in the face of the terrible threat from Kichibei's army. To Kamari, that bandit was one of Kichibei's soldiers, carrying his wife away to be enslaved, tortured or executed, and so he acted in accordance with these emotions, and did whatever was necessary to protect the one he loves.

It was now full dark and we had not yet reached the location where the wolves held council. Matai had sent runners ahead, but, so far, we had received no word back. The moon was barely visible through the thick leaves above and cast little or no light in the forest around us. I was worried how easy it would be for Kamari or I to trip on an exposed root and twist an ankle or walk into a tree in this impenetrable darkness.

An owl hooted hollowly in a tree above as it watched our odd party pass beneath it. Other than that, the only sound was the wind shifting the leafy boughs over our heads, blending with the gentle rustling as a wolf brushed its thick fur against a brother in the dark.

We must be nearly there by now... I thought tiredly. As if he had heard my thoughts, Matai spoke:

'Not long now – we're almost there,' he called from the front of the group without turning his head. 'In fact... here we are.'

For a few moments I could still see nothing in the darkness other than the ever present and indistinct shapes of the trees around us. Then, up ahead, I discerned a break in the trees. A clearing maybe? But as we drew closer in the wan light of the moon, I realised that this was no simple clearing. Passing through the edge of the trees, the wolves ahead spread out around an unseen perimeter and stood waiting. At last we stood abreast with them and the sight that lay before us took my breath away. We were standing on the rim of an abandoned sandstone quarry and ranged out in every hollow, on every ledge, were several hundred wolves, every pair of amber eyes focussed upon us. The quarry was not particularly large; it had the look of a place that had been mined extensively for a short period of time before the workers had moved on or been forced out, but the sight was no less impressive.

At the centre of the quarry sat a lone wolf. He was large indeed, larger even than Matai, and from the tip of his snout to his tail ran a distinctive stripe of black fur. On his left shoulder were three deep and obvious scars which he seemed to wear like a badge of honour. He seemed to beckon me towards him – even though he made no obvious movement – and I found myself stepping towards the rim of the quarry and beginning to slide carefully down to the bottom, with a perplexed Kamari following close behind. At each ledge I reached, the wolves around us parted to allow access to the wolf at the centre, who watched our every move. When at last I reached the bottom, both Kamari and I were covered in dust and panting heavily and – although I cannot speak for Kamari – my heart was racing, whether from fear or some other emotion I am not sure.

I felt very small under the watchful eyes of the wolves around us, but I remembered the importance of the task I had been set and swallowed my nerves, stepping towards the wolf as boldly and proudly as my fatigued legs would allow.

'So, you are the two Lord Orran has sent to ask us for aid,' the wolf said in a deep throaty growl that Kamari of course could not understand. 'Takashi Asano and Kamari Shiro.' I nodded in answer but did not say anything. I could sense a powerful air of authority from this wolf and deemed it best not to speak until bidden to. 'My name is Jaroe, I am the leader of this Council. It has been many months since we last checked in on the affairs of the Kurai; our Council has run far longer than we expected it to, but that was beyond our control... Tell me, what has been happening these past months that demands our attention?'

I looked hard at Jaroe for several seconds before answering. Beneath his outwardly calm and composed exterior, I could sense his anxiety and his loyalty; they carried in every word he spoke. It was very different from when Matai spoke to me on this matter. From him, I had sensed impatience, even anger, at the message we had brought. The possibility of a divide in the Council now seemed more obvious, and forbidding.

I was deeply perplexed. These wolves were supposed to be the guardians of Hirono, of the Kurai, and they knew nothing of what had occurred over the last few months. I could only conclude that the subject of their Council had been of supreme importance for it to distract them from their duties for so long. But what could be so important as to divert their attention away from Harakima and the fight against Zian?

'Then… then I take it you know nothing of the return of Zian Miyoshi?' I asked tentatively. 'About his theft of Orran's Blade and his attempt to overthrow Lord Orran and claim Hirono as his own?'

A gasp ran through the surrounding wolves, snarls and angry voices rose into the night air.

'What!' Jaroe almost yelled in shock and rage. 'And he is still at large!?'

'No, no, no,' I replied, struggling to make my voice heard over the wolves around me. 'He is dead. I… I killed him, but that is not why we need your aid, well… not directly.'

'Silence, all of you!' Jaroe snarled fiercely, his voice echoing around the quarry, spreading instant quiet. Turning back to me he said, 'tell me everything you know.'

And so, I told him everything, beginning with my earliest knowledge of Zian's movements which had been the attack on Morikai Village while Kamari was visiting his aunt and uncle. From there I continued our story, tracing the route of Zian's mercenary army as best I could, describing the path they had ploughed through Kirina and my own village, Aigano.

I detailed the events that occurred at Harakima including the attack Zian's army staged on the front of the castle, so Shjin could escape with the Blade over the back wall. I explained that Shjin had only stolen the Blade under duress; his family had been held captive by Zian and his dual loyalties to both his family and his lord had all but driven him to madness, practically tearing him in two.

I told him of the reconnaissance party sent to investigate Zian's fortress and discern his strength, and explained that when it returned, it was no longer a party. Only one man, Gorobei Iesada, had survived, but their investigation had uncovered that the enemy numbers were not sufficient to repel the full strength of the Kurai. However, Orran is a cautious man and so a messenger had been sent to Toramo Village to ask for aid. When it was discovered to be deserted, Orran was left with no choice but to send in only what he had - the full complement of the Kurai - and hope that Gorobei's information proved to be correct. He knew time was short and they had to act quickly before Zian could release the dragon, Aralano, from the Blade.

I related – in as much detail as I could remember – the journey to Zian's Fortress and the discovery of Tiramai Village trapped in perpetual winter, completely destroyed by the might of the dragon, who we realised with horror had been released.

And then of course came the battle itself. The unprecedented and horrendous loss of Kurai warriors affected the wolves deeply as they listened. I replayed in my mind the entire battle for them, recounting the treachery of Gorobei and his lies about the enemy strength. I related how the Kurai had teetered on the brink of destruction before Daisuke Inaba – a Kurai warrior initially suspected of stealing the blade – appeared with the Toramo warriors and an army at their back, swaying the tide of battle in our favour.

And then there was the battle with Aralano himself, where even more brave warriors were lost – including Meera. I told them how Aralano had at last been killed and how I had pursued Zian into the castle, where I at last caught and killed him, almost dying myself.

At last I had reached the reason Kamari and I had come all this way to ask for their aid. I explained all about the threat from Lord Kichibei, who had caught wind of the Kurai's vastly depleted numbers and seen his chance to finally reclaim Hirono. I told them that – for all I knew – his army could be on Harakima's doorstep right now.

'Lord Orran had nowhere else to turn, and he had heard I could speak to wolves, so he asked me to seek you out and implore you for aid,' I finished.

Commotion broke out among the wolves and a division amongst them was now a certainty. Everywhere I looked there were wolves turning on their neighbours, their voices clashing together in a battle of wills. The sound was deafening; snarls, growls and yelps of anger filled the air and through all this commotion Matai walked calmly towards the centre of the quarry. He came to a stop beside Jaroe, who I could see quite clearly was struggling to stop himself from running to Harakima on his own, regardless of what the majority of the Council might say on the matter.

Matai tried to make his voice heard over the hubbub, but none of the wolves paid any attention. Without warning Jaroe pointed his nose to the night sky and howled. It was a long and piercing sound that rattled the ribcage of every wolf close by, a sound that demanded the attention of all who heard it. The uproar died down slowly as Jaroe's howl ran on and on until at last he ended and silence reigned.

'Now,' he began, glaring at all the wolves staring back at him. 'You all heard what Takashi had to say. Lord Orran and the Kurai need our help and we are honour-bound to do everything in our power to aid them. I know some of you are less than happy about this, but in times past there would have been no question and I do not see why there should be any now.'

'With all due respect Jaroe,' Matai said at his ear. 'Times have changed and we have never had a problem of our own as dire as the one we now face. Let us not forget that we have lost our new Soul Channel...'

CHAPTER SEVEN

Matai paced up and down in front of Jaroe, who was looking at him as though seeing him for the first time.

'Matai,' Jaroe said slowly, a definite edge to his voice. 'It is our sworn duty to protect Lord Orran and keep the peace in Hirono. There is no discussion to be had here. The Soul Channel will have to wait.'

Matai ceased his pacing and glanced around at the wolves lining the quarry ledges.

'Why should we help them?' he burst out, bringing a snarl to Jaroe's lips. 'Why should we help them when they cannot help themselves? For generations our Council has watched over this domain and rather than grow stronger, they have instead needed our help more and more frequently. The Kurai spirit is waning, it is a shadow of what it once was; they have become weak and complacent, relying on us to rescue them from every hardship. Why should we aid those whose spirits no longer glow as brightly as their ancestors?'

Anger swept through me at Matai's words. The Kurai had fought body and soul for their lord in the battle at Zian's Fortress – even when defeat seemed certain and all hope had faded – and he had the audacity to say that the Kurai spirit no longer burned brightly? He had not even been there to fight alongside them. No, he and the rest of his Council had shirked their duty to discuss their precious "Soul Channel," whatever that may be.

Matai did not seem to sense my anger; at any rate, he did not say anything about it. It was clear that he had wanted to say this to Jaroe and the others for a very long time, and Kamari and I had given him just the excuse he needed.

'The Soul Channel must be our prime concern – the Kurai will have to take care of themselves for the time being,' Matai said, self-righteous confidence evident in his tone and his feelings. 'Once we have retrieved the Soul Channel, then… then we can return our attention to the Kurai once more.'

'You are not the leader of this Council,' Jaroe snarled angrily. 'I am, and no one wolf ever decides its path. It must be put to a vote; we will let our brothers decide and I hope they will remember where their true loyalties lie.' Jaroe stood up and moved several paces to Matai's right where he sat down again. 'Choose then, my brothers,' Jaroe said loudly, his voice echoing around the quarry. 'The path of self-continuance, or the path of duty and honour.'

Silently, the wolves leapt down from their ledges and made their separate ways towards the centre of the quarry. There they split and began to form groups behind the two wolves. I watched as many a guilty look crossed the face of a wolf as they passed by Jaroe and took their place behind Matai. But for every one that looked guilty, there were three I could tell were pleased this day had come and the words they themselves would not dare to speak had finally been said.

When the last wolf had made their choice, the scale of the division was at last laid bare. It was an almost exact half and half split, as far as I could guess, and my heart sank at the sight. What on earth were we going to do? We could cut our losses and go – leave the half of the Council who had chosen Matai and head back to Harakima; but even as I thought this, I immediately dismissed it. Half of the Council simply would not be enough to repel Kichibei's forces. Somehow, we had to unite the Council and we had to do it quickly, or Harakima would be overthrown and Kichibei would seize control of Hirono.

It seemed clear to me the only way to end this dispute was for someone to retrieve their Soul Channel, but if the Council had been discussing this problem since before Zian's appearance, then the solution must be desperate, difficult or out of their reach. I could feel myself being pulled deeper and deeper into this, but time was dreadfully against us and someone had to do something – what choice did I have?

'Tell me what happened to your Soul Channel,' I said, my voice passing through the tension that crackled on the air, 'and I will do all I can to find it for you. It seems the only way to resolve this.'

Jaroe broke off the furious glare he had aimed at Matai and turned to look at me, a strange light gleaming in his eyes and a feeling of hope radiating from him in waves.

'I see it now...' he said slowly, calculatingly. 'This is why you were sent to us. It is in you that we must put our faith. You are the one who can bring the Soul Channel back to us and put an end to this divide.'

Matai had crossed the gap between the two groups and stood next to Jaroe, a probing look on his face.

'Yes, yes... I see it now too...' he said, staring at me intently. 'Let this boy set out to retrieve the Soul Channel, let him prove to us that the warrior spirit still burns in the Kurai – that there is something to save should we go to Orran's aid.'

'But, I am not truly Kurai – I was not raised in their culture...' I answered uncertainly.

'You lived among them for many days, did you not?' Jaroe asked.

'Yes,' I answered simply.

'You made friends there, integrated into their society...'

'I... I suppose...'

'You learned and absorbed their culture, you fought and bled alongside them,' Jaroe continued. 'It is not about where you were born or where you grew up, it is not even about your skill with a blade. You embody everything that they stand for.' Here Jaroe broke off for a moment and looked at me almost proudly. 'You are Kurai,' he finished, and Matai nodded fervently at his side.

I had never considered myself as Kurai before now. So much had happened at Harakima and after that I had never taken the time to really think about it.

'Yes,' said Jaroe, nodding as though confirming something to himself. 'It is you who must do this. You asked what has happened to the Soul Channel, but before we tell you that we must first explain to you what it is. The knowledge of its history will impress upon you the importance of this to our Council.'

Jaroe glanced at Matai, who took a deep breath and began pacing up and down in front of me, his amber eyes gazing off past the trees and towards the sky.

'The Soul Channel has always been with us, in one form or another,' he began slowly. 'It is said that the first Soul Channel came into being through a warrior, the greatest warrior ever to have lived. He fought many battles in the south, stemming the tide of a bandit lord who threatened to break through Agrath's Deterrent, the vast wall that divides the northern domains of this land from the south. He went on to found a village somewhere in the north, but unfortunately his trouble with the bandit lord was not yet over. Other battles were to come, and they would eventually lead to his death.'

This story sounded strangely familiar, but try as I might I could not recall any major details or where I might have heard it. For some reason my memories of it seemed hazy and unclear, as though a fog had settled over my thoughts and all I could focus on was the task at hand.

'After his death his soul did not pass from this world,' Jaroe said, picking up the story. 'He received a blessing from the spirits and his soul remained here where it formed the Soul Channel - the means by which a strong warrior's soul can be channelled from his corpse to the skin of a wolf. The Soul Channel then went searching for a strong line of warriors, worthy of this great gift, and it was in the Kurai that it saw this worth.'

'Many lords from across the land have sought to uncover the root of this gift and harness it for their own,' said Matai, taking up the story once more.

'Or destroy it,' Jaroe put in angrily.

'But none have ever come close until now. Our Council ran on far longer than expected because it was the time of the Transference; our old Soul Channel was fading and the gift – as it always is – was passed to another. But shortly after arriving and taking up the gift, our new Soul Channel was stolen from under our noses by a lord from the south named Higai.'

'That is one of the most disturbing things about your story,' said Jaroe. 'I cannot know for certain, but it seems possible that Zian may have planned his attacks knowing full well that we would be here holding Council. How he could have learned this I do not know, but if true, he could have passed this information on to

Lord Higai. It is no secret that Higai has always sought to steal our gift and if he was successful, it would only be good news for Zian, as it would keep our attention distracted from his activities...'

'Then what is keeping you here?' I asked mystified. 'Why not head for Higai's province and retrieve the Soul Channel?'

'Because Higai's men did not take it back to Hinjai, of course,' replied Matai. 'They took it somewhere they knew we could not follow.'

'Where?' I asked, fearing the answer.

'An island off the western coast,' Jaroe said darkly. 'The one place a wolf cannot follow them, for – as you can see – we are ill equipped to sail a boat,' he finished, holding up a forepaw, a humourless smile creasing his face.

'This is of the utmost importance, Takashi,' Matai said seriously. 'We fear greatly for the safety of the Soul Channel. We fear they may find some way to take this gift for themselves or – failing that – destroy it, and we cannot allow that to happen. The Soul Channel is the beating heart of this Council – without it, no more wolves will be born to us and our Council will soon dwindle and die, leaving Hirono a darker and more dangerous place for everyone... You do understand the importance of this?'

'I do now,' I answered, nodding my head. 'If I am to retrieve this thing then tell me what it looks like.'

'You will know it when you see it, it will be another test of your spirit,' Matai replied cryptically.

'If you do not see it for what it is then you were never the one to have reclaimed it and we made a mistake putting our faith in you.'

'Wolf, what is going on?' Kamari whispered in my ear, startling me. I had almost forgotten he was standing right beside me; I felt so singled-out by the events that had unfolded that I had almost convinced myself I would be facing them alone.

'I will tell you in a minute,' I whispered back, his expression betraying the obvious anxiety in my voice. 'So how are we to get to this island?' I said, turning back to Jaroe.

'I will lead you to Port Asukai,' Jaroe replied. 'It is about a day's walk away on the western coast. From there you will have to find a boat that will take you to the island.'

'But… we do not have any money, we have no way to pay for our passage,' I said anxiously.

'We cannot help you with that,' Matai cut across Jaroe. 'You will just have to work something out yourselves; try appealing to the captain's better nature.'

'But if this Soul Channel is so important and powerful, then Lord Higai will have set many men to guard it, how are we supposed to retrieve it?' I asked, feeling the first stirrings of panic as I pictured Kichibei's army marching ever closer, our window of time to prepare growing ever smaller with each passing second.

'No more questions,' Matai growled as he moved to shoo us out of the quarry. 'This is a test of you, of

your spirit. Reclaim the Soul Channel and we will
unite and help you, or do not, and shatter both our
hopes and our faith.'

Before I knew what was going on, Kamari and I
had been hurried out of the quarry by a contingent
of wolves with Jaroe leading us on. I barely had time
to brush the dust from my clothes before we found
ourselves alone in the forest again, the Council of
Wolves disappearing like puffs of grey smoke.

'Follow me and by tomorrow morning we will be
in Port Asukai,' Jaroe said over his shoulder as he
began to walk west through the early morning mist.

'Kamari, look,' I said, pointing at a familiar shape
trotting cautiously towards us through the trees.
Dagri came to a stop in front of me and nuzzled my
clothes, his ears flicking from side to side so fast, it
was as though they had a life of their own. I patted
his flank and checked the saddle bags again to make
sure they were still tight. Taking his reins in my left
hand, I began following in Jaroe's wake.

'Wolf, please tell me now – what is going on?'
Kamari asked worriedly, putting a hand on my
shoulder as he walked alongside me.

'I'm sorry you couldn't understand any of that,
Kamari,' I began, looking at him seriously. 'Because
there was a lot to take in. I will explain it all to you,
but what it boils down to is this – we have another
task to complete before the full Council will come
back to Harakima with us…'

CHAPTER EIGHT

As we walked, I related everything the wolves had told me about the Soul Channel to Kamari, including of course our part in returning it to them. Half stunned, Kamari munched on a piece of bread that was beginning to go hard, digesting this information as he digested the dry bread that made me thirsty just looking at it. We would have stopped to make ourselves a hot meal, but Jaroe wanted to press on, telling us we could eat properly once we reached the port.

'So... you and I... together... alone... are to go to this island and retrieve this Soul Channel from an unknown number of armed men?' Kamari asked dubiously.

'Yes,' I replied simply. 'And we must be quick about it or we may return to Harakima to find nothing but a smoking pile of rubble.'

'And this is meant as a test of your spirit? Of the Kurai spirit?' he continued. 'And it is in you – or should I say us – that they have put their last great faith to achieve this goal?'

'Yes,' I answered again.

Kamari massaged his forehead perplexedly as he thought about this and everything it entailed. Finally, he lowered his hand and shrugged his shoulders.

'Well… I suppose there's not much point moping and moaning and asking the spirits "why me? Why was I chosen?" This is what needs to be done and we have been tasked to do it, so together we will accomplish it… or die trying,' he ended resolutely.

'I knew I made the right choice bringing you along,' I said with a laugh, bringing a smile to his face. 'Whatever I may face on the path set before me, I would have no other by my side.'

Kamari gave a grimace of mock disgust.

'Are you trying to make me bring this bread back up?' he asked, giving me a shove and laughing heartily. 'Less of the sentimentalities.'

Jaroe had said nothing since advising us to eat on the move and press on to Port Asukai, so I signalled for Kamari to stay a few paces behind, handed him Dagri's reins, and sped up to match pace with the wolf. After a few moments silence I spoke.

'So, I take it that Matai has been causing problems for you and the Council?' I asked. Jaroe was silent for a few moments as though considering how best to answer this. Then he sighed deeply and replied.

'It may have appeared that way to an outsider,' he began solemnly. 'But every member of the Council has felt as Matai does at some point, even if – in the end – loyalty wins out. We have guarded this domain and the Kurai for more years than I care to mention and we have all felt the decline in their spirit. Our numbers were once many times what they are now, but recently fewer and fewer Kurai warriors have been deemed worthy to join our Council.'

Jaroe fell silent and I could feel his sadness and anxiety like waves of heat.

'My loyalty to the Orran line and the Kurai still burns in my breast,' he continued. 'It will never leave me and I will always jump to aid them if possible; but in many of the other wolves this loyalty has dimmed and they look now to the continuance of our Council, and that hinges on retrieving the Soul Channel. For them it is their one and only concern, and unfortunately Orran will just have to wait until we have solved our problem.'

'But surely the Soul Channel and the Kurai are inherently linked?' I replied. 'If Higai's men manage to harness this gift – or if they destroy it – then no more Kurai Wolves will come into being and the Council will fade; but if the Kurai are wiped out by Kichibei's men because you would not go to their aid then… either way, your Council is facing extinction, whether sooner or later.'

'I know, I know,' said Jaroe with another sigh. 'I hope you understand that this is not what I wanted to happen.' He took a deep breath and looked off into the west. 'I do not believe for one second that Higai's men will be able to harness our gift, but there is a very real chance that they will destroy it in anger and frustration and if they do, then our Council will fall. Put simply – if we do not save the Soul Channel, we *know* we are doomed. If we go to Orran's aid, we will also face being wiped-out in battle and then *still* return home to this same problem. Most of the Council would rather save themselves from extinction than rush to help Orran once more and risk everything.' He glanced here at the startled and angry expression on my face. 'But you heard what Matai said. Basically, what this comes down to is that many of the Council feel the strength of the Kurai spirit is all but gone and there would be little to save should they run to Orran's aid once more. That, I believe, is the main reason they refuse to go with you until the Soul Channel is returned. So, it is upon you and your friend now that everything rides. I believe the Kurai spirit still burns bright, and in the battles ahead, I know that will be proven; I just hope the Council has united by then and converged on Harakima, so Matai can see it for himself...'

'It is an incredible gift that has been bestowed upon you,' I said after several minutes of silence.

'Yes, it is,' Jaroe said with a smile that showed all of his jagged teeth. 'And we plan to hang on to it for as long as possible.'

'In your past life, you must have been a great warrior to receive this gift and rise to the head of the Council,' I said interestedly. 'What was your name before...?'

'We do not talk about our old lives,' Jaroe cut in, not angrily but firmly. 'It is in the present that we live, Takashi… not the past. Let us focus on our problems of the moment, and leave the past where it belongs.'

Ahead of us stretched a daunting span of undulating green fields, but thankfully we had just crested a hill that afforded us our first decent view of the sea, a shimmering bluish-grey band that spanned the horizon. I had never seen the sea before, having lived my whole life in Aigano, and I was looking forward to discovering as much as I could about it in the short time we would have to get acquainted.

Kamari seemed strangely cheerful as we hurried along a good ten paces behind Jaroe. I could not understand his mood given all that lay ahead of us.

'You seem considerably happier than most would be in your situation,' I said lightly.

'I was just wondering how I would have felt about myself if I had not come with you,' he replied. 'Not that Ellia would have let me stay, of course,' he added with a grin. 'But I don't think I could have lived with myself – knowing I was sitting there doing nothing while there were people out there fighting so that I could go on sitting there doing nothing.'

I raised my eyebrows at this remark.

'I can't imagine you ever sitting doing nothing,' I said. 'Particularly when there's the chance of a fight,' I added with a laugh.

'I was just thinking – and this is what made me happy – I was thinking that sometimes it's just nice to know you've made the right choice, that you're on the right path or the path that is right for you. It's just… it's a comforting feeling to know you've made the correct decision – morally and spiritually – a decision you will never feel guilt or shame over, a decision you can be proud of,' he said, his voice trailing off. 'It just… it made me feel happy,' he finished.

Night had crept up on us. A chill breeze blew across the field and above the gentle rustle of grass I could just about hear the leathery wingbeats of bats, flitting about and snapping up any flies unfortunate enough to cross their paths. In the inky darkness, the glow of torchlight from the Port was clearly visible, giving us a beacon upon which to set our sights. Asukai still seemed a good distance away but at the pace Jaroe had set us – even if we stopped for a couple hours' sleep – we would be there by morning. By this point I was so tired I was close to collapse, but even in this state, I knew I still would not sleep tonight. I would not know another night's sleep until I found her again. That I was certain of.

Kamari handed me a flask of water from which I drank deeply, splashing a little on my face to try and dispel the grogginess that pervaded every inch of me. Kamari was holding up admirably, but I could see how badly he needed a few hours' sleep. If it had just been he and I, then I would have called for a rest, but in Jaroe's presence I felt it best to allow him to dictate when and where – or even if – we rested.

'Your friend looks as though he might fall asleep standing up,' said Jaroe, as though he had read my thoughts.

'I wouldn't put it past him,' I said with a smile and a sly glance at the bone-weary Kamari. 'I've seen him fall asleep whilst swimming before.'

Jaroe let out a bark of laughter.

'Then I think it would be best if we stopped for a while and let him get some sleep.'

'Thank you,' I replied, turning to my friend to tell him this. Kamari gave what I can only describe as a delighted grunt and hurried ahead to a small wooded area.

By the time Jaroe and I got there, Kamari was already asleep, his raucous snores disturbing the birds that were roosting above him. He had not even bothered to unroll his sleeping mat and had simply thrown himself on the floor at the base of a tree and fallen instantly into a deep slumber.

'That's a remarkable gift he has,' said Jaroe with a tired grin.

'You have no idea,' I replied looking down at his sleeping form as I tethered Dagri to a tree. 'If I could only sleep half as easily as he can, it would be a blessing.'

'Well, I think it would be best if you at least try and get some sleep,' said Jaroe. 'I will keep watch and wake you both in a few hours.'

'Thank you,' I said again, unrolling my sleeping mat and slumping down near Kamari.

It was closer now. I could sense it. I had not yet opened my eyes, but I knew that it was very close by. What did it mean? Why did I keep seeing it?

I opened my eyes and looked up into its face. It was leaning over my prone form, staring straight into my eyes. The wolf that I had seen on two previous occasions – the dark, shadowy wolf that had haunted my thoughts for days – was now so close that I could reach out and touch it. I looked past the wolf at Jaroe, who was facing the opposite direction, apparently unaware of the creature standing over me.

I looked back at the wolf and saw that it was gazing unblinkingly at me. In this wolf I saw memories – many of my own but also many from a past that was not mine, but felt familiar all the same, and I felt a power; a power I now felt throbbing in my veins, giving me new strength.

Its mouth did not move, but for the first time I heard its voice, clear and authoritative, ringing inside my head. It spoke but a single word.

'Hurry.'

And with that it was gone, vanishing like a ghost, and in its place now stood Jaroe looking down at me.

'Come, Takashi, rouse your friend, we cannot afford to rest any longer,' he said.

We had reached the port at last and even at this early hour, there were still people going about their business in the flickering torchlight as though it were midday, their voices ringing out across the cobbled streets. From where we stood on the edge of town, I could see the half-lit shapes of boats tied up at the dock, their many and differing sizes and designs fascinating to me. I could hear the dark sea water slopping against the hulls of the boats and I could feel a sea breeze blowing against my face and taste the salt on my tongue.

The town itself was small, consisting only of a few tiny inns and bars and several houses where the dock workers lived, as well as three or four storehouses where the goods from the boats would be unloaded. The buildings themselves were simple wood and tile affairs, homely and serviceable, but a clear indication that this was a working town and not a place in which you would choose to raise a family.

We had already decided that the best place to start looking for a captain to ferry us to the island would be the bars. The bars were where sailors would inevitably flock to, after long weeks at sea, to gather all the latest gossip from land and drink their troubles away.

'Here is where I part with you,' Jaroe said in an undertone, feelings of anxiety, hope and shame radiating from him. 'I only wish I was able to come with you, but I think a wolf in your party might draw the wrong kind of attention to you. The thought of going back to the Council to sit and do nothing, while you two risk your lives… I am caught between two groups here and I do not know how long I can stand it, I…'

Here he stopped and I felt his anxiety and helplessness flow more strongly from him. I found that I was reminded forcibly of Shjin Kitano when I had come across him in Zian's fortress – wounded and bleeding – a broken man who had been caught between his duel loyalties to his family and his lord.

'I… I wish you the best of luck,' he continued, 'both of you, and I do not wish to pressure you further, but I feel that I must – I beg you to return to us as swiftly as possible so that I will not have to sit idle for long.'

I nodded in acknowledgement of his plea; there was no middle ground here.

'We will return to the Council in time,' I said stoically. 'Harakima will not fall to Kichibei's forces.'

After a short pause in which Jaroe studied me, he said simply:

'I believe you.'

The wolf turned his head and nodded at Kamari who returned the gesture wordlessly. Without a sound, Jaroe spun around and within seconds had disappeared off into the darkness.

'What did he say?' Kamari asked quietly.

'He feels ashamed that he is not able to come with us and help,' I replied, still looking at the early morning shadows into which Jaroe had vanished. 'And he wished us both luck in what lies ahead. Come on, we need to find a captain and we need to do it quickly.'

After tying up Dagri in a secluded area, we went in search of the bars. The first one we walked into was deserted other than the barman, who did not look up as we entered and simply stayed where he was, drying a wooden cup with a rag. He was an extremely aged man with huge bushy eyebrows and a mane of white hair that fell to his shoulders. He wore a long, faded blue kimono that was well-worn, but had clearly been quite magnificent in its early days. The overpowering smell of rice wine filled the air of the small, dim bar, catching in my throat and making me cough.

'Excuse me,' said Kamari, walking over to the barman. 'Do you know where we might find a captain to take us to the island nearby?'

The old man looked up at Kamari slowly and raised his eyebrows so that they almost vanished into his hair.

'A captain? At this hour of the morning?' he replied croakily.

'Yes, it is vitally important, and we are in a terrible hurry – do you know where any might be, please?' Kamari insisted.

'You might try the bar across the street, that's where most of the captains drink,' he said. As we turned to leave, the man added, 'I hope you're prepared to pay through the nose for their services, most of them don't come cheap.'

'What are we going to do?' I asked once we had exited through the sliding door of the bar. 'We don't have any money.'

'I'll think of something,' Kamari replied distractedly. 'Maybe we can find someone loyal to Orran who can help us.'

Hurriedly, we crossed the street to the bar the man had indicated, but when we got there, we found that it too was deserted, but for its barman. This man, much younger than the last, directed us to go back across the street to the bar we had just come from, as it, likewise, was, "where the captains usually drink".

'We just came from there and we were told that *this* is where the captains drink,' Kamari said exasperatedly. The barman shrugged and continued to dry the wooden cup in his hand.

'Well, as you can see, business is not exactly booming this morning,' he said in a voice that made it quite clear the conversation was over.

Back outside, Kamari ran a hand angrily through his long, dark hair and looked quickly around, as though expecting to see a captain come striding towards us along the dock.

'Shh, do you hear that?' I asked, listening intently.

'What?'

'Voices, listen…'

And voices they were, separate from the voices of the dock workers we could see unloading the ships nearby.

'There must be another bar close-by,' I said optimistically. 'Come on.'

We followed the voices and soon the slurred speech became obvious, so we knew it must be a bar that had some customers. Reaching it at last, we saw that the sliding door was wide open and across the doorway hung a split cloth curtain that bore the symbols for "bar" and "open" on it. The glow of candlelight from within and the *clunk* of wooden cups drew us inside.

The bar was almost full. Many men were seated cross-legged around low wooden tables, the surfaces of which were hidden by the myriad jugs of rice wine they had consumed. As we entered, every head turned to look at us, suspicion and hostility evident on most faces, their eyes scanning our bodies and coming to rest on the swords we each wore.

'Excuse us,' Kamari said loudly and commandingly. 'We are looking for a captain to take us to the island out to the west. Is there anyone here who will help us?'

With grunts and angry mutterings, the men turned back to their tables, waving their hands dismissively at us.

'We have been sent here by Lord Orran,' Kamari continued unperturbed. 'Our task is of dire importance, is there not one man here who owes allegiance to Orran? Not one man among you who would help us?'

'Get out of here!' one man yelled drunkenly, making a feeble attempt to throw his cup of rice wine at us. The cup shattered on the floor several paces from us.

'How dare you!' Kamari yelled, putting a hand to the hilt of his blade. 'We come here asking for aid in the name of Lord Orran and you dishonour yourselves – all of you!'

He took a step towards the man, but I held him back.

'We may find ourselves a bit outnumbered if you start anything,' I whispered in his ear, glancing around the room.

Kamari let his grip on the sword handle loosen and I turned on the spot to check the far corners of the room. As I did so, a middle-aged man caught my eye. He was sitting alone at a table in a darkened corner and was surreptitiously beckoning us over.

I tapped Kamari on the shoulder and pointed in his direction. Together we walked over to his table and took a seat opposite the man, who was now pouring out rice wine for each of us.

The man looked considerably older than he probably was; most likely the result of a hard life at sea. His hair, which was tied up at the back, had clearly once been coal black, but was now streaked with grey and his beard was long and unkempt. His skin looked to have an almost leathery texture and his eyes were deep-set and full of life. He wore a plain cream kimono belted with a black sash and wooden sandals on his feet.

'You are Kurai, yes?' he said, his voice carrying a strength you would not think was there to look at him. Kamari and I both nodded. 'What are your names?'

'I am Kamari Shiro and this is Takashi Asano,' my friend said without hesitation.

'Ah, I recognise your names; you must originally be from Aigano, yes?'

'Yes,' Kamari answered, and I heard the pride in his voice that he had for once been recognised for his lineage.

'My name is Takai Muraki,' the man said, drinking his cup of rice wine in one swallow and placing it back on the table. 'I am the captain of a small cargo vessel docked here. It is nothing special, but I believe it would serve your purposes adequately.'

'You will help us?' I blurted out.

'Most assuredly,' Takai replied with a small smile.

'The thing is… the problem is…' I began awkwardly. 'We do not have any money to pay you with…'

'That does not matter, I will not ask you for payment,' Takai answered.

'Why not?' asked Kamari suspiciously. 'Why will you help us?'

'Well, believe it or not, I was once Kurai too,' he replied, catching us both off guard.

'You were Kurai?' Kamari said in surprise. 'What happened? What are you doing here?'

'Ahh, it was many years ago now,' Takai began slowly. 'I was dismissed from Lord Orran's service and somehow… I ended up here.'

'Why were you dismissed?' I asked interestedly, only realising after how rude the question was. Luckily, Takai did not seem offended by the question.

'Well, it is a matter of deepest shame, but I understand and agree with my lord's decision,' he said, thinking back to the day it had occurred. 'I was on guard duty on the walls of Harakima. It was my youngest son's birthday, but I had not yet seen him that day as my duties had kept me constantly busy. It was a quiet night, no threats had been levelled against us, and I decided to leave my post and sneak home to see my son for an hour or two. About an hour after I left my post, a group of bandits attacked the area I had been guarding. They raised ladders and managed to gain the wall-top and kill several men before they were brought down by our archers.' Here Takai sighed and rubbed his eyes. 'I was prepared to be commanded to commit ritual suicide, but instead it was worse. My family and I were banished from Harakima and after many months – and far too many false starts to count – I became a fisherman, living out of this port. I've never forgiven myself for what I did. Since we left Harakima, I've lost my wife and my three children are spread across the land – gods only know where. But I always agreed with Orran's decision. I made a grievous error of judgement and he was right to banish me, so I still owe him my allegiance, and if I can help him by helping you, then I will do whatever I can to aid you.'

CHAPTER NINE

I felt huge respect for Takai in that moment. Even after everything he must have been through since being banished from Harakima, he still felt honour bound to Lord Orran. I was about to thank him for agreeing to help us when a loud, drunken voice rang out from a table nearby.

'You're going to help those two young whelps for free, Takai? Did I hear that right?'

It was a youngish man, maybe in his thirties, who was sitting at a table across from us. His words were badly slurred, almost unintelligible, but the tone was unmistakable. It was spiteful and condescending, so much so in fact that I felt my hand reaching unconsciously for the hilt of my sword.

'Are you going soft in the head, old man?' the drunkard said into the silence that had fallen across the bar. 'How do you know what they're saying is true?'

Kamari and I stood up simultaneously, both of us reaching for our swords. At the same time the men at the table opposite got to their feet menacingly, their faces red from too much drink, their eyes watery and unfocussed but angry. Takai stood up and stepped between us, trying to placate both parties at once.

'Gentleman, there is no need for anyone to get upset. Tamoe, let me buy you and your friends another drink,' he said to the drunkard as he reached for his money pouch. Takai had taken a step closer to Tamoe while searching for his money. The drunken man reached out and slapped the pouch from Takai's hands, sending coins skittering across the floor.

'I don't want your money, old man,' he spat.

I just managed to restrain Kamari before he drew his sword, but it was close.

'Come on,' said Takai to Kamari and I. 'It is the drink in them talking. I think it would be best if we left.'

I had to drag Kamari out backwards as he was still facing Tamoe determinedly, his eyes locked fiercely on the other man's.

Once outside, the early morning breeze helped calm us a little, but Tamoe's disrespectful and uncalled-for comments still made my blood boil. Takai could clearly see how angry we both were.

'Pay them no mind,' he said, studying us closely in the last of the moonlight. 'When they drink that much, it truly brings out the worst in them. Being at sea for such long periods of time can do strange things to the mind but, trust me, next time we see them they will be full of headaches and apologies.' Kamari looked on the verge of storming back into the bar and smashing a wine jug over Tamoe's head, so he added quickly: 'Follow me and we will load up my ship for the journey.'

Takai owned a small stable next to the storehouse he kept his goods in and invited us to leave Dagri there, where he would be safe. Once we had tethered Dagri in the stable, with enough feed to last him a few days, we began to load up Takai's ship with food and other supplies. The ship itself was not particularly large; Takai told us it was mainly used for making deliveries up and down the coast and that it was unsuitable to be taken far out to sea. When we looked at him worriedly, he alleviated our fears by telling us that the ship could easily manage the journey to the island, it was only if it was taken out on the open ocean – where there were much larger waves – that there could be a problem.

In the east the sun was beginning its ascent into the sky and from all around came the sounds of the port inhabitants waking up to a new day. Seabirds wheeled and called over our heads and the rigging of the ship creaked in the breeze. Kamari and Takai were on the ship ahead of me, stowing supplies in the cabin as I struggled towards them, weighed down by a heavy coil of rope.

I did not hear them approach as I was concentrating intently on not tripping over my burden. The first I knew of their presence was when a hefty fist collided with the back of my head, sending me staggering forwards. I tripped over the rope I had been carrying and hit the cobbled street face-first. Warm, dark blood gushed from my nose and down my chin as I tried to sit up, my head feeling as though there was a battering ram inside. A large and blurry figure came stumbling towards me, fists raised, ready to strike me again. From my prone position I caught the tang of rice wine on the wind and knew at once it was one of the men from the bar – probably Tamoe. He was almost upon me, leaning down to pummel me again, but even in my semi-conscious state, I found that I was prepared. I allowed him to get so close that I could smell his rancid breath before I brought my foot into play, kicking upwards into the man's chin and clacking his teeth together painfully. He went down hard onto the street, clutching at his mouth and giving me time to roll away from him and struggle to my feet.

I tottered along the dock towards Takai's boat, but I was in so much pain that really, I did not know in which direction I was walking.

'Kamari!' I yelled. 'Takai!'

It was then that I sensed something behind moving rapidly in my direction. I pricked up my ears and found that I could hear it, clear as day. It was an object, not a person, travelling speedily towards my head, whistling through the air. I threw myself down and heard it hiss past my ear where it smashed on the cobbles a few paces from me.

Kamari must have heard this because his footsteps came hurrying towards me and I discerned his anxious shouts.

'Takashi! Takashi!'

I felt his hands on my arm as he helped me to my feet. Swaying groggily, I rubbed my sleeve across my nose to stem the flow of blood.

'Where are they?' I asked, looking blearily around, but Kamari had gone quiet and still and did not respond at first. Then he glanced around us worriedly.

'Come over here,' he said quickly, leading me towards a wooden barrel filled to the brim with rain water. I dunked my head into the ice-cold water and tasted the iron-like tang of blood. I pulled my dripping head out and ran my hands through my hair, trying to clear my vision. This swift break had helped but had not stopped the hammering in my head. I turned to look at whatever Kamari had seen and spotted the six men from Tamoe's table advancing towards us, Tamoe among them. They were not armed, but if they all punched as hard as Tamoe just had, it would not matter.

'They're still drunk,' Kamari whispered to me. 'We can use that to our advantage, their balance and aim will be completely off.'

Kamari drew his sword, but I put a hand on his arm to stop him.

'No, they're just drunk,' I said, my voice sounding strange through what was probably a broken nose. 'No swords, I do not want their lives on my conscience.'

The fight that followed was swift and brutal. Kamari had been right, the men were so drunk that afterwards I was surprised Tamoe had actually managed to hit me in the first place, and had not simply swung at thin air. That is not to say that Kamari and I did not receive any injuries. By the end, Kamari's lip was bleeding badly after one of the men unintentionally hit him with an elbow while attempting a punch, and I was covered in bruises.

The six men, however, were far worse-off. Kamari had managed to send one of the men sailing into the dock and the man had somehow – miraculously in his drunken state – managed to pull himself out of the water before he drowned. Each one of them now lay on the street, cut, bruised and groaning; their injuries adding to the thunderous hangovers they would soon be experiencing. Many people had gathered to watch the fight, but now it was over they were just milling around, none of them leaping to help the downed men. I got the impression that perhaps they were not well-liked by the locals.

Turning our backs on them, Kamari put his arm around my shoulders and led me over to Takai's ship. I was limping again after one of the men stamped on my foot and aggravated an old wound, so our progress was slow. Takai had taken the opportunity to finish loading up the ship, so by the time we arrived we were ready to get underway. Before we set off, Takai cleaned and checked the wound on my nose and assured me it was not broken. After checking the wound to Kamari's lip, we set sail from Asukai dock.

The boat was so small that Takai was perfectly able to sail it on his own, meaning that Kamari and I were free to roam the ship and take in the sights, smells and sounds of life at sea. Neither of us had ever been on a ship before and we knew very little about them. Kamari was extremely interested in the actual sailing of the ship, the furling and unfurling of the sail, the way the rudder was used to turn the boat and catch the strongest breeze, so he spent most of his time speaking with Takai at the wheel. I, on the other hand, was content to stand at the prow, alternately watching the waves below slapping the side of the ship and scanning the horizon for the island we were heading for.

In the distance I noticed an area of water that was glittering strangely, the sun's rays lancing off the waves more than usual. As we drew closer, I saw that it was a shoal of silver fish just below the surface that scattered in every direction as we passed. As I watched I spotted a large, dark fin break the surface of the waves, heading towards the fish that were fleeing before our boat. I caught sight of pitiless black eyes, a gaping crimson maw and a flash of teeth, before the water began to boil as the predator tucked into its feast. From only a short distance above, I viewed this spectacle in awe. It was like nothing I had ever seen before. As quickly as it had begun, it ended. Fin, the name I later remembered it by, moved off and vanished beneath the waves, its hunger staved-off for now.

I had not been listening to the conversation between Kamari and Takai as I had been so wrapped-up in my own thoughts and the sights around me, so when I did start to listen, I realised that Kamari was telling him the details of our task for Lord Orran.

Perhaps if we had made our business for Lord Orran clearer to the men in the bar, they may have been more willing to help us, but it was not something I felt comfortable discussing in public. Takai was different, however; I felt that I could trust him implicitly. It was an instinctual trust, like I had felt for Shjin when we first met. We could not have stumbled upon a better person to help us in our hour of need.

It was early evening by the time Kamari finished conversing with Takai and came to stand by me in the prow. Wordlessly, he handed me a dumpling and began chewing on one he had brought for himself. After a while he spoke with his mouth full.

'If you had asked me in Aigano where I thought I would be at this point in time,' he began, spraying crumbs everywhere. 'I can say with absolute truth that a boat somewhere at sea is the last place I would have thought of.'

I did not respond to this, for there was something far more important on my mind I wanted to discuss with him. But he had already denied my suspicions once, so there was no reason to assume he would suddenly divulge his secret to me now... However, I felt I had to try.

'Kamari,' I said, turning to him seriously. 'Tell me what it is you have been hiding from me ever since we left Aigano.'

There was no denying it. When he answered, he definitely could not meet my eyes.

'I told you last time, Wolf, this is all in your head – there is nothing I have not told you. Just drop it, will you?'

The colour had risen in his cheeks and his voice wavered slightly. I knew that he was lying. Whatever it was, I guessed it must be worrying or shameful for him. But were we not brothers? What could possibly be so hard for him to tell me, his best friend? I wanted to press him for an answer – force him to tell me what he was keeping from me – but something inside, something instinctual, told me that now was not the right time. Everything happens for a reason, I reminded myself. The reason behind this feeling that prevented me from questioning him further would become clear in due course, and when it did, I might not like what I discovered.

I walked away from Kamari without a word and as I did, I caught a sound I probably should not have been able to hear. A slight sigh, under his breath; a barely suppressed expression of unvoiced emotions, and in that moment I realised that the secret he was hiding from me was not hidden by choice. He wanted to tell me his secret, but something was preventing him – some oath or threat that only time would reveal. So, I would wait, and when the time felt right, I would ask him once more and he would tell me, and only then would I discover whether it would not have been better kept a secret.

'We're here, boys – Shika Island.'

It was barely distinguishable in the fast-fading light, but there it was – the island we had set out to find, the island no wolf could reach, the island where the Soul Channel was being held… Takai had spotted it first, calling Kamari and I up to the wheel where we would have a better view of our destination. The dull glow of firelight could be seen on the far side of the island, but from this distance it was impossible to tell how many people might be there.

'I think it would be best to get as close as we can to the island and then wait until the dead of night to land,' I said, looking up at the sky and studying the distance between us and the island.

'Agreed,' said Takai. 'They seem to have set up camp on the north-western coast, so I presume they will have docked their boats there too. As soon as it's fully dark, we'll sail for the southern tip and land there.'

'Alright, then Wolf and I will go ashore, but Takai… we will need you to wait here for us,' said Kamari apologetically.

'Of course,' Takai answered with a smile. 'You didn't think I would leave you here, did you? We just need to find somewhere out of sight to land the boat.'

'What if they find you?' I asked anxiously.

'Don't you worry about me,' Takai replied. 'Focus on what you came here for.'

As we spoke, our boat continued to drift serenely towards the island, buffeted along on a light sea breeze, cutting through the path of light the rising moon had painted on the waves.

'There is no way we can plan for what is ahead,' Kamari said to me gravely. 'We have no idea of their numbers or the layout of their camp and, to be honest, neither of us actually knows what it is that we're looking for… All we can do is play it by ear and bide our time until we find what we came for, and the moment is right to strike.'

I nodded mutely. The enormity of the task before us had welled up inside once again, threatening to overwhelm me. However, the sight of Kamari standing at my side gave me the strength to swallow my fear and concentrate on what had to be done, and the reason we were doing it.

It was approaching the Spirit Hour – the hour after midnight when the ghosts and spirits of our land are most active – and it was now dark enough for us to make land with less fear of discovery. It was considered bad fortune to be up and about during the Spirit Hour and, generally, I would respect them enough not to be outside at this time; but this was no ordinary situation and we had no time to waste. We would just have to take our chances and risk angering the spirits in order to complete our task.

It was eerily quiet as we approached the southernmost point of Shika Island and prepared to dock. We were entering a sheltered cove and the trees that grew nearby overhung the water, making it the perfect place to hide the boat from view. Close by, we could hear waves lapping up the beach and smacking against rocks, while above us, the trees rustled and swayed in the wind.

Takai threw the anchor overboard and the rope creaked loudly as it pulled taut, the noise sounding as loud to me as a yell. We had been lucky. The cove we had chosen to stop in was practically a natural dock and Takai swiftly had the ropes tied to various roots and outcrops to secure the boat in place, leaving enough slack to take into account the rise and fall of the tide.

My heart was thudding painfully fast in my ribcage and I could hear it horrifyingly loud in my ears. After tying-off the last of the ropes, Takai gave a short bow to Kamari and I – a sign of respect for us and the mission we were embarking upon. He used this gesture in place of words, for he then vanished silently into the cabin. It was clear he was worried about us and – like Jaroe – he wished that he was in a position to follow us, but given Takai's age and physical state, he would be more a hindrance than a help.

Nodding to each other, Kamari and I slipped over the side of the boat into the freezing water, holding our weapons above our heads, and began to wade ashore. We had not brought any food with us as we wanted to travel as light and fast as possible; and anyway – if we took so long on this island that we needed to eat, then we might as well just turn back now. We had, however, brought a flask of water each, which we had tied to our belt sashes.

At last we made it to the beach and stepped out of the icy waves, our clothes now thoroughly sodden and weighing us down – our feet sinking easily into the damp sand.

'We head north,' said Kamari, the leader in him coming to the fore once more. 'A single sound could be the death of us, so be careful and watch your step. We will get as close as we can to the camp and then assess our options from there, but it will be down to you spot the Soul Channel for what it is.'

I gripped my sword handle tighter as I nodded in agreement.

'Do you think Takai will be alright?' I asked, trying not to focus on my own fears by thinking about someone else.

'He'll be fine, it's us I'm worried about,' he replied grimly.

Together we made our way north up the beach towards the centre of the island, which was covered in dense woodland. From our position I could see a small range of rocky hills to the north-west and I pointed these out to Kamari.

'From there we would probably have a good view of their camp,' I said, once Kamari realised where I was pointing.

'Good idea,' he replied, changing course slightly.

We reached the trees and disappeared into the shadows, the firelight glow from the opposite side of the hills dying down as morning drew ever closer.

CHAPTER TEN

I had thought that by this point in my life, I would have a better handle on my fears and anxieties, but as we walked through the dense forest, faces from my imagination leered at me from every tree and shadow. Every branch became a clawed hand reaching out to grab me. Every snap of a twig an enemy at my back. I saw figures from my childhood nightmares materialise before my eyes – creatures of myth and legend that were used as bedtime stories to make naughty children behave. In the shape of one tree I saw Sarlai, the night demon, a spindly figure of shadow and vapour with piercing, blinding white eyes, who came to take away the souls of children who did not say their prayers and pay their respects to the spirits. In another I thought I saw Tiera, a vengeful nature spirit, whose form changed depending on the crime needing punishing. Tiera dealt with children who did not show the proper respect for nature, like killing animals for sport instead of food. It was said that a child who had angered her would awake one morning to find their hands sewn together, so they would never be able to kill for fun again. I knew these were just stories – with no basis in fact – but they had always terrified and delighted me in equal measure.

The wind stirring the treetops sounded hauntingly like laughter, and the branches that had been trying to grab me now seemed to be pointing mockingly, as though in deepest contempt for the seemingly impossible task we found ourselves faced with. I looked over at Kamari ploughing on through the forest – stoically silent – never allowing his imagination to get the better of him like I did. He was always so focussed on the present, so single-mindedly dedicated to whatever he was doing, whereas I… I was always off somewhere else, and now, more than ever, I needed to focus on the task at hand. But it seemed that this was my way of dealing with difficult situations – by thinking about anything other than what I was doing. Everyone handles fear in their own way and this… this was my way.

I had begun to lag behind Kamari again. Several paces ahead, he had stopped at the base of a beech tree, staring intently at the bark. When he turned to beckon me over, his expression was apprehensive and upon seeing this, I hurried to see what he had discovered.

There were markings on the trunk of the tree – unintelligible words and symbols that had been carved deeply into the bark with a jagged weapon and the indentations were painted in with…

'Blood…' Kamari said in a whisper, after touching one of the pictures that looked horribly like a flayed human body.

'I wonder who carved these…' I said slowly, my voice barely audible.

'I don't know, but what I do know is this… we are not alone in this forest…'

After that we ceased all talk, and if we had to communicate, we did so by hand signals. We moved slower now, creeping as silently as shadows through the dead leaves and fallen branches that littered the ground. The signs of life were now more obvious and pronounced. I noticed piles of ashes where fires had been lit and the further we progressed, the more gruesome the signs and symbols around us became. On one tree I saw the body of a squirrel nailed to the trunk, its belly slit and dried blood spattered across the ground beneath it. Nailed to another tree was a bird, plucked bare of all its feathers, its eyes staring sightlessly into the dark.

Whatever was living in this forest was more primal and brutal than anything I had encountered before, even more so than the barbarian mercenaries Zian had brought with him from overseas. They clearly showed no respect for nature and it made me wish the story of Tiera was true, so that she would come and deal out retribution upon these people. From what I could see, whenever they stopped to make camp and light a fire, they put up these carvings and dead animals to mark their territory and ward-off intruders. Their behaviour seemed ancient, ritualised, the product of a bygone era when small tribes roamed these lands, shunning all outsiders. It seemed clear to me that these symbols were saying "this is our land – you are not welcome here", but we had no choice; we had to pass through this forest to reach the hills. We just had to hope that we could slip by unnoticed…

It was almost morning and the sky above was lightening, but deep within the forest it remained as dark as it had been at night. For the past hour or so we had not heard a single sound; no birds or animals seemed to live in this part of the forest. Clearly, they had seen the signs too and wisely decided to steer clear of it.

'Stop, what's that up ahead?' Kamari said in an undertone, holding out an arm to halt me.

'What?'

'That there. See it? At the base of that tree?'

'No.? Wait… I see it. What is that, is it a…?'

Stealthily, Kamari began to approach the tree. Away to my left I spotted something too and began to creep towards it, a cold chill spreading throughout my body. In the shifting shadows of the forest it was difficult to make anything out clearly, so I approached the object cautiously – hoping it was not what I thought it was. My foot caught on something solid that shifted as I made contact and I fell forwards, throwing out my arms to break my fall as quietly as possible. I sat up quickly and turned to face the thing I had fallen over. What I saw at my feet made my skin crawl, as though hundreds of insects were moving about inside me.

I had to look away to keep myself from yelling or vomiting. I was not surprised I had not seen the object that tripped me. It was human, but every inch of visible skin was covered in dark wood ash to camouflage it, only its dead white eyes stood out in its face. It was a male and he was almost skeletally thin, his ribcage clearly visible beneath the skin. Looking at him lying there, I had to admit that my first thought was that I had stumbled over the Sarlai, lying in wait for me. As I took several quick, shocked breaths, I realised there was a gaping wound in his stomach that had clearly proved fatal and I could tell from the dry, crusty blood that he had been dead some time. The ground, however, was sticky underfoot and I shuffled backwards, away from the corpse.

Behind me, Kamari gave a muffled yelp as he made his own grisly discovery. I turned and saw another skeletal figure, with skin blackened by wood ash, pinned to the base of a tree trunk by a primitive looking spear. *Killed with his own weapon*, I thought to myself.

A breeze kicked up then, carrying with it the rank smell of death, making me splutter and gag. Looking around – the shock helping my eyes adjust – I saw that there were bodies everywhere, but it was only as the sun finally rose above the horizon and the first feeble rays of light fell to the forest floor that we were truly able to take it all in – the debris, churned earth, and myriad criss-crossed footprints that marked the site of a battle…

A tiny noise – a rustle maybe – somewhere close by, grabbed my attention. My hearing seemed to sharpen of its own accord and suddenly I could hear things I knew I shouldn't be able to. Kamari's muttering and murmuring from ten paces away seemed infinitely louder, as if he was shouting in my ear. I could hear a stream somewhere to the north, even though I could not see it. And the sea, which we had left behind some time ago, I could now hear once more with perfect clarity. But cutting through all of these I could hear the sound of…

I just had time to dive to one side as a spear hissed out of the tree foliage above and thudded into the blood-spattered ground, followed swiftly by a roaring, snarling figure covered in wood ash and leaves. Weaponless, the crazed creature launched himself at me as I lay on the ground, gnashing his teeth and clutching at my throat, seeking to bite out my wind pipe.

'Kamari!' I yelled in a strangled voice as I struggled to fling my assailant from me.

Kamari was already running towards us with his weapon drawn. I managed to unlock the creature's hands from my throat, but as soon as I did, it began scratching at my eyes and I bellowed in pain as it scored several deep cuts down my cheeks with its long, jagged nails. I stared into its bright white eyes and saw again the Sarlai, demon of my nightmares.

Suddenly its hands went limp, a slight gasp escaped its lips, and it fell forward onto me. In its place I saw Kamari standing over me, blood dripping from his blade, his expression full of concern. I threw the body from me and sat up, my face fiery with pain.

Kamari tore a strip from his haori, a half-length coat, and began to dab at the wounds on my face. I could feel warm blood sliding down my cheeks and dripping onto my clothes. In a daze, I sat there quietly as Kamari tended my wounds, using some of the water from his flask to clean them.

'You have got to stop injuring your face,' he said with an effort, trying to make me smile. 'I don't know how much more it can take.'

Despite myself, I wanted to laugh, but it would have hurt too much to do so. As I sat there, I knew most people in my position would have felt angry with this creature for attacking, but looking at it, I felt pity instead. Over centuries of isolation, this race of people had honed their instincts down to the basest of needs and desires, a razor-sharp focus on survival. They lived simply, and one of their simple requirements to live was that they should be left alone by the outside world. Clearly, the men who had stolen the Soul Channel had stumbled across them, and someone had started the fight. And the evidence was all around us that the primitive people had lost the battle.

'Can you stand?' Kamari asked after a while. 'I'm sorry to do this but we cannot stop to rest any longer, we must press on immediately.'

'Yes, I can stand,' I answered with a painful smile. 'It was my face he scratched not my legs.'

Kamari gave a grunt of laughter and helped me to my feet. We began walking north-west again, picking our way through the scene of the battle; the bodies, the debris and the blood. As we passed, I could not help but feel sorrow; sorrow for this unknown, invisible tribe who no longer existed because Lord Higai had decided to try and take the Kurai's gift for his own.

It was close to midday and we had almost reached the rocky hills. We had spent the last few hours in silence, although I had noticed Kamari glancing at me when he thought I wasn't looking.

'Are you sure you're alright?' he asked at last, putting a hand on my shoulder and looking into my face.

'I'm fine,' I replied hollowly. 'These will heal,' I said touching a hand to the red-raw scratches on my face, 'it's just that… I'm… I'm tired.'

'You haven't been sleeping, have you?' Kamari asked after a pause. 'That's why you always went on first watch when we camped.'

'I haven't slept properly since she left and I… I just feel like I'm coming apart inside,' I answered dully. 'I need to find her because… because I need her, and because I need to sleep.'

I was not sure whether Kamari understood this, but I could tell that he desperately wanted to help me in whatever way he could.

'We agreed that when we found each other again we would run away together,' I said. 'Just run, and see where our legs took us, but now I feel that if I find her again, all I will want to do is sleep.'

'Then, when this is done, we will find her together,' Kamari said, clapping me on the shoulder. 'And you will find out whether you will run or sleep.'

We had reached the base of the rocky hills and began the ascent to the top, where we could view the movements of the enemy in their camp. It was a slow and dangerous climb up a steep, scree-covered incline. Every so often, one of us would slip and a mini avalanche of dirt and pebbles would threaten to drag us down the hillside, where we risked being impaled on the jagged rocks below.

On one occasion Kamari slid past me in a wave of shale and dust. Thinking quickly, I grabbed a spur of rock and threw out an arm to grab him, gripping his hand tightly and holding on until the hill had settled once more. He had cut his leg quite deeply in the fall, right along the shin bone. I tore a strip from my haori this time and bandaged his leg after cleaning it with some water.

'We haven't even spotted the enemy yet and look at us both,' I said with a laugh.

It was late afternoon by the time we crested the top of the hill and were finally afforded our first sighting of the enemy. We were both dusty and sweaty and breathing heavily. We sat down just out of sight of their camp and drank deeply from our water flasks. When we had caught our breath, we peered out over the ridge together.

A band of trees lay between the base of the hills and the camp, which was situated on the north-western beach of the island. Beyond the camp, the ships the men had arrived in lay at anchor and beyond that the sea stretched on to infinity, blank and featureless, looking as calm and flat as a piece of slate.

The camp was a haphazard arrangement of tents and supply crates, roughly dotted around a central meeting area. This meeting area comprised a circular arrangement of rough-hewn logs around a large pile of ash that drifted and danced on a strengthening sea breeze. Set apart from the others was a much larger tent, inside of which several figures could be vaguely discerned moving around. Elsewhere, the camp was alive with activity – there were men sparring, some cooking over small fires and more still talking in groups everywhere we looked.

'There must be at least sixty of them,' Kamari said in a whisper as he watched the camp's movements. 'Maybe more on board the ships or foraging for food.'

I scanned the camp carefully, feeling the pressure of time clamp down on me worse than ever. I knew I would have to identify the Soul Channel before we could make any plans on how to reclaim it.

'Can you hear what they're saying?' I asked my friend without looking at him.

'From this distance, no one could hear them,' he replied.

I was about to agree with him when it began to happen again. Unbidden, uncontrolled, unknown – my hearing seemed to sharpen. Like a strong wave approaching a beach – building in intensity – I heard their voices grow louder in my ears and I began to make out what they were saying to each other. In and amongst the other voices, two seemed to filter to the surface.

'…much longer are we going to be here?' I caught one man saying to a comrade.

'Don't know,' his friend replied. 'No one but Hanjo really knows. We'll be here as long as it takes for him to understand and control the power of this thing for Lord Higai.'

'What is it about it Lord Higai wants so desperately?'

'Don't know that either,' his comrade said again. 'But you must have felt it? There's just something about it that… I don't know. It just makes me feel strange, like… like I'm looking back in time or something.'

It was then that I heard it, stabbing through my core more painfully and more penetratingly than any arrow ever could. It started low and steadily grew; grew and grew and grew to a height of piercing emotion I had never before believed possible.

A howl…

'Hurry!'

In that instant, everything became clear. Terrifyingly clear. This was why she had left. This explained the nature of the inexorable force that had torn her from me. She was the Soul Channel! It was Meera!

My head reeled, thoughts racing round my mind like a whirlwind. It had never occurred to me that the Soul Channel might be a creature – to be honest, I had not given it much thought. Back at the Council, the wolves had mentioned something called the "Transference". Clearly Meera had been summoned to become the next Soul Channel, and no matter how hard she tried, she had been unable to escape the summons. Their previous Soul Channel had been waning and Meera had been called to take its place, only to be captured by Higai's men shortly after arriving…

Meera! It was her. I knew it. I knew it as certainly as I stood on this hill, but more than that, I felt it – deep inside. She was here, close by. I had found her again at last!

I had no recollection of moving at all. One second, I was sitting on the ridge with Kamari, watching the camp. The next, I found myself scrabbling down the other side of the rocky hill, frantic in my efforts to reach her. I felt a strong hand clutching at me, gripping the back of my haori and clinging on. I struggled violently, wriggling like an eel to free myself, but the hand that held me was far stronger than I.

I thrashed around – my eyes never leaving the tent from which the howl had emanated – as I felt myself being hauled back up the hill and over the ridge. The dust I was kicking up swirled around me and I coughed and spluttered as it entered my eyes and mouth. I felt a pair of hands settle on my shoulders and a concerned face moved in close to stare at me.

'Wolf, Wolf! You have to calm down! You are not going to help her by getting yourself caught,' the face said. But I could not listen to this person. Did he not realise that Meera was right there, in that tent! Why wouldn't he let me go? I had to get down there and help her! I squirmed harder than ever, but still could not move an inch.

'Wolf, it's me, Kamari. You have to listen to me, you know that I'm right. This is not the way to help her.'

Something in his voice got through to me and pulled me back. I stopped struggling at once and lay still, panting heavily, the howl still reverberating in my head. *Hurry!*

'I'm sorry, Kamari,' I said at last, looking into his face and seeing the worry there. 'I don't know what came over me, it's just that... it's her, it's... it's Meera...'

'I know,' he said gently. 'Look, I have a plan, and as far as I can see, it may be our only chance. We just have to wait until nightfall...'

CHAPTER ELEVEN

The world seems so much different at night. Shapes and structures appear strange and unfamiliar when blanketed in shadow and – as evidenced by my experience in the forest earlier – the darkness has a habit of playing tricks on my mind. But I could not afford to lose focus tonight. I had to try not to let my imagination run away with me – Meera depended on it.

Kamari and I had crept further down the hill and were crouched amidst the trees that bordered the camp, directly behind the tent in which Meera was being held. Bats flitted overhead in the gloom, standing out starkly against the star-filled sky. I had an ominous feeling about the plan Kamari had laid out for me – there was just too much that could go wrong – but we had very little choice.

My hearing definitely seemed sharper. I felt far more attuned to my surroundings than ever before, almost like an animal. It was strange and frightening for I could discern the exact locations of the guards merely by sound, their footsteps pounding like drumbeats in my ears. But with these inexplicably heightened senses came again the stark feeling of inevitability; an outcome which I could not escape, nor wanted to. It was like a rope was tugging at the very centre of my being, pulling me along a path, making my decisions for me. This feeling unsettled me deeply because I had no idea of its origins or its direction, and I feared it might lead me away from Meera.

It was bitterly cold and the men guarding Meera's tent were seated around a blazing bonfire nearby, only getting up to check on her once every few minutes. After watching the camp for over an hour, we were fairly certain that – other than Meera – the tent was indeed empty. So, once we were inside, we would have a few minutes to release her and escape before the guard came over and noticed her absence.

We made ready to go. I drew my short sword from its scabbard and weighed it in my hand, my eyes trained on the guards seated by the fire. After a few moments one of the guards stood up resignedly. He stretched mightily and yawned before making his way over to the tent.

'Get ready,' Kamari said in my ear as the guard moved stiffly towards the tent, lifted the flap, and glanced inside.

'Go,' whispered Kamari.

Together we moved off silently towards the back of the tent. We heard the sound of the guard shuffling grumpily back to his fire and made our move. I slipped my blade under the fabric of the tent's back panel and slit it open, creating a gap large enough for us to pass through. I hurried inside and stopped in anger and sorrow at the sight that met me.

Meera stood with her back to me, her large ears swivelling around at the sound of our entrance. She had been cruelly tied in such a way that she could not comfortably lie down and was forced to stand upright day in, day out. Each of her four legs was tied to a separate stake and a rope around her neck was tied to another. She looked gaunt and dreadfully tired but as she turned to me, restricted as she was by the ropes, I saw again my love. In those eyes I saw myself, standing on the battlement of Zian's Fortress as she came to me and professed her love. I saw her passion and excitement as she told me her desire to run away together. Right then I saw through her exterior to the woman I had fallen in love with; the woman who had saved my life by sacrificing her own.

'Oh Meera,' I whispered brokenly.

I went to her and put my arms around her as Kamari moved quietly to the entrance, his weapon held ready. Grasping my sword firmly, I began to cut through the thick ropes around her neck and legs. The need to be quiet slowed my progress and as each taut rope finally snapped, I winced, fearing the guards would hear. My fears were well founded.

'What was that?' I heard one of the guards by the fire say to a comrade.

'What was what?'

'I thought I heard something in the tent...'

'It's just that wolf. If you had to stand up all day you'd fidget too.'

'Well, I'm going to check on it again anyway,' the first man answered.

'Suit yourself, but you're wasting your time,' the other man replied. I heard the man get up and make his way towards the tent.

'Someone's coming,' I whispered to Kamari as I began to frantically chop through the second to last rope.

'I know,' he replied quietly. 'Hurry!'

But we did not have enough time. I was now on the last rope, but the guard had reached the entrance to the tent. Kamari raised his weapon. In the darkness I saw that his face was set and determined, an iron-strong resolution to protect his friends – he had indeed become a true leader.

The main flap of the tent raised as the guard poked his head inside, sending a patch of flickering firelight across the floor to illuminate Meera. She stood now free of the ropes, her hackles raised, a growl rumbling deep in her throat – softly but menacingly. Kamari brought the hilt of his sword crashing down on the guard's head, knocking him unconscious and dropping him to the floor like a stone.

'Jikao?' one of the guards seated by the fire called. 'Jikao, are you alright?'

'Move!' I whispered to Kamari and Meera, ushering them to the gap at the back of the tent. 'Let's go, let's go!'

Within moments we found ourselves deep amidst the trees that skirted the base of the rocky hill we had stood upon earlier. Angry yells and shouted commands rang out from the camp behind us as Meera's kidnappers swiftly roused themselves and gave chase. It appeared they knew this island well, for they were gaining on us and there was little we could do to stop it. Meera had clearly been tied in that cruel way for several days; her muscles were weak and she had already begun to lag behind.

I considered carrying her, but she would slow me down so much that we would only be caught anyway. I could not believe that we had come so far only to be caught at the very point I was reunited with her. It seemed there was nothing else for it. It would be a fight to the death…

They were ahead of us now. Somehow, they had cut in front of us to block our escape. We were heading in a southerly direction, but if we continued on this path they were sure to catch us.

'Go east,' I shouted above the sounds of our enemies rushing ever closer through the trees. We veered off to our left – branches whipping our faces and bodies – and sprinted on to the base of the hill, our hearts in our mouths. We reached the hill and began to climb. This was our only chance. There was no escape. All we could do was gain the high ground for the battle to come.

I looked down at Meera. She was panting heavily and her limbs were shaking with fatigue. My heart went out to her and my fury at these men increased tenfold. How could they have done this to her?

Morning seemed to have crept up on us fast and already the first tentative rays of the sun were feeling their way down to earth. In the weak grey light I spotted the first of them, running full tilt from the tree cover towards us. Their comrades were not far behind, appearing in a line spread out at the base of the hill. Early morning mist clung to their clothes and swirled around them as they began to advance up the slope towards us, their weapons drawn and raised.

As they drew closer, I could see the men's eyes were trained on Meera's fangs, which she was showing in a bloodcurdling snarl. They seemed far more afraid of her than our blades. Kamari, Meera and I stood side by side on the rocky hill – blades and fangs facing the enemy. My foot slipped on the unstable ground and I just managed to keep my balance as the fight began.

Our enemies were highly-trained and fought well, but being roused from their beds at such an early hour had thankfully thrown-off their timing. Many of our foes were bleary-eyed and sluggish, but there were also some – the night guards mainly – who were alert and battle-ready. A burly guard with a dark, scraggly beard took a vertical slice at me with his blade, which I deflected, throwing him off balance enough that I was able to kick him backwards, sending him tumbling down the hill into his comrades.

At my side, Meera leapt back, snarling, as a misjudged swing at Kamari whistled past her nose. With a howl she launched herself at the man, latching onto his sword arm and biting his wrist to the bone. With an agonised scream, the man vainly tried to shake her off as his blood welled up in her jaws, but Meera's grip was like iron and she would not let go. It was only when a comrade jabbed at her with his sword that she released the man and let him collapse to the ground, cradling his mutilated arm.

Being the strongest of our group, Kamari as usual felt duty-bound to protect us and seemed to have bitten off more than he could chew. He was faced with four men who were slowly but surely battering him into submission, forcing him to parry one punishing blow after another. I threw a fist into the face of the man closest to me and pushed him back into his comrades as I struggled over to Kamari.

Upon reaching my friend, I crouched low and swung my foot out, catching the nearest of his attackers in the back of the leg and bringing him hard to the ground. I lashed out with my foot again and sent the man sliding down the hill, watching as he collided with several other men, tripping them. Kamari's attackers turned to look at me and that was all he needed to off-balance two of them and send them hurtling backwards. I hacked at the other man with my blade, but he skilfully parried every blow. However, his concentration had been fixed on me and so he did not see the loose stone that caused him to lose his footing and crash to the ground, his head cracking against a rock and knocking him unconscious.

'Stop this!' a voice shouted out above the tumult, loud and commanding.

At once, all movement amongst the enemy ceased. They lowered their weapons and backed-off, but not before Kamari had shoved the man closest to him down the hill. He raised his weapon and prepared to leap after his quarry when the voice rang out again.

'I said, stop this at once!'

Even Kamari stopped moving this time, but he did not lower his weapon. The men below us parted to allow passage to the man who had spoken. A tall man stepped into view and approached us slowly. He was dressed in wide crimson hakama trousers and a cream haori coat and appeared to be unarmed. His black hair was tied in a knot on the top of his head and his face was clean-shaven and youthful.

He stopped several paces from us and, to our surprise, bent his head in a bow to us both. He had an intelligent look about him and I did not see in him the threat I had seen in the guards watching over Meera.

'My name is Hanjo Matsui,' the man said in a polite and formal tone that caught me completely off-guard. 'What are your names?'

Kamari and I were so taken aback by this new development that for several seconds we could say nothing. After sharing a confused look, Kamari took a step forward.

'I am Kamari Shiro and this is Takashi Asano,' Kamari said eventually. 'But he is known as Wolf.'

Hanjo stared at me for a few moments as though he were studying or appraising me. It was unnerving; it felt as though he were looking into me. Then he nodded and swept his gaze to Kamari.

'My first question would have been "what are you doing here?" but you have already made that abundantly clear,' he said, with something approaching a smile. 'So instead I must ask you what your intentions are in escaping with this wolf?'

I was bruised, I was achingly tired, and I could not be bothered hiding the truth of our task from these men. Chances were that if we failed in our task, then the consequences would affect them anyway. Maybe they could be reasoned with.

'We were sent by Lord Orran to gather an army to fight-off the approaching threat from Lord Kichibei's forces. As far as I know, they are currently on the march to Harakima to reclaim a domain he believes is rightfully his,' I said wearily, watching Hanjo's face as he digested this information.

'And... how does this wolf in any way relate to that?' Hanjo asked.

'Lord Orran sent us to request aid from the Council of Wolves, guardians of the Kurai. I presume you know of them as you have been holding its most important member captive,' I added, unable to keep the cold fury out of my voice.

For a minute or two Hanjo said nothing. He simply stood quiet and still, clearly thinking deeply.

'Ahh, I see,' Hanjo said after a time, nodding to himself. 'The wolves will not help you fight off Kichibei until the Soul Channel is back in their possession. That is why you are here, correct?'

'Correct,' I replied venomously.

'I know what you must think of me,' Hanjo said, looking into my face. 'I know the wolves are worried for her safety and I can see that you are too. They were worried that if... *when* we failed to gain the gift, we would kill her, but let me tell you that she has not been harmed. I would never allow any harm to come to her.' He paused briefly when he saw that I wanted to speak, but continued before I could begin. 'And before you say it, the way she was tied may have appeared cruel, but it was the only way we could think of to keep her from escaping again. She may be a little weak for a while, but no actual harm has been done.'

I did not know what to say. This man was not how I imagined the thief of the Soul Channel. He seemed wise, intuitive, and keen to preserve the wellbeing of Meera. He also seemed to have the uncanny ability to answer my questions before I asked them.

'You may already know this,' said Hanjo, taking our silence as a cue to explain himself, 'but we were sent here by our lord, Higai, to study and gain knowledge of the link between the Kurai and the wolves. Our task was – not necessarily to steal – but to harness this great gift that has thus far only been bestowed upon the Kurai. We had known of this gift for many, many years, but it was not until a source came along with invaluable information on the Soul Channel and her whereabouts, that Lord Higai ordered us to find her. We would not normally act on information from a source we did not trust, but Lord Higai was terribly eager and the information appeared in-depth and genuine.'

It must have been Zian, I thought to myself. *Zian must have been their source*. He had planned everything, from his occupation of Hirono onwards. He had wanted to completely ruin the Kurai. By giving details of the Soul Channel to Lord Higai he had hoped they would either steal the gift from the Kurai or destroy it in frustration. Either way, he won.

'After several difficult months, we were finally able to capture the Soul Channel – unharmed – and transport her to this island where the wolves could not follow. We have been studying her fruitlessly ever since,' Hanjo finished, his eyes fixed in honest fascination upon Meera. 'So, may I ask why you two were sent out to round up an army when Lord Orran has a great many, shall we say... *older* Kurai warriors at his disposal?'

'The Kurai army is not what it once was,' Kamari replied guardedly.

'You have heard of Zian Miyoshi's attempt to occupy Hirono with an army of foreign mercenaries?' I asked.

'I have heard rumours,' Hanjo replied gravely. 'But as I said, we have been working on the acquisition of the Soul Channel for many months now, I am a little out of touch with goings on elsewhere in the land.'

'Well, the battle with Zian left the Kurai army severely depleted and the deterrent of Orran's Blade has been eradicated,' Kamari explained, a hard edge still apparent in his voice.

'Lord Orran sent me to the Council of Wolves to ask for their aid because... I am able to speak their language,' I added, acutely aware of how closely Hanjo was now scrutinising me. 'And, although many of them were willing to help Lord Orran at once, there are many who will not aid us until the Soul Channel is recovered safely.'

'I see,' Hanjo said, rubbing a hand thoughtfully along his jaw, the same slight smile tugging at his lips. 'And you expect us to simply hand over the Soul Channel to you?'

CHAPTER TWELVE

Kamari glared furiously at Hanjo, his hand straying to the sword he had only recently sheathed. However, my reaction did not mirror Kamari's. I could sense something about this man – a compassion and understanding that was rare in these times. I could tell that he trusted everything we had told him, even if the other men around us did not believe a word of it. The evil men I had imagined to have stolen the Soul Channel had turned out to be just that – imagined – for Hanjo seemed to be a man simply following his lord's orders, and doing so according to his own upright sense of morals and principles.

'You know as well as I that Lord Kichibei will not stop with the fall of Harakima,' I said earnestly. 'His army will sweep across Hirono like a sickness. He will seize control of the entire domain, then push south beyond Agrath's Deterrent until you find him on Hinjai's doorstep. Your home will be taken from you and your lord put to death.'

'Then what is to stop us joining forces with Kichibei?' Hanjo asked, still smiling slightly. 'An alliance with him could prove most fruitful.'

'And how long do you think an alliance like that would last?' I countered. 'Long enough for them to use you before putting you all to the sword. From what I have heard, Kichibei is a greedy and ambitious man who would rather conquer a province than ally with it.'

'I would not side with Kichibei even if my lord ordered it,' Hanjo said quietly. 'I would take my own life before then. We have always had an understanding with the Orrans. Though we envied their gift, we have never once had a conflict and this land has known peace for many years, thanks to them. I would gladly side with Lord Orran to fight-off a threat such as Kichibei.'

'Then we need your help,' Kamari said, stepping closer to Hanjo. 'We need to take Meera – the Soul Channel – back to the wolves so they will fight with us. But even with their help, it may not be enough. So, I ask you – implore you – to join us as well and help defend Harakima.'

'This gift you sought to extract from the Soul Channel,' I said, taking over from Kamari. 'It was a gift bestowed upon the Kurai for being great and courageous warriors – they did not get it for nothing. Fight with us and maybe, somehow – if the spirits will it – this gift will be granted to your people too.'

'Sadly, I doubt that to be true,' Hanjo answered slowly, his brow creased in thought. 'The Soul Channel is bound to the Kurai – they were chosen, and they alone. I cannot see this gift being shared.

But... as you say, maybe, somehow, it could happen – if the gods and spirits deem us worthy.'

Hanjo looked at us intently for a few moments longer; Kamari, Meera and I standing side by side, facing-down a small army that had the power to snuff-out our lives in an instant. Our fate lay in the hands of the man who had taken Meera away from the wolves – away from me. After several minutes standing stock-still, Hanjo seemed to come back to life.

'We will return with you to Harakima,' he said at last. Gasps and angry mutterings could be heard from several of his men. 'My Lord Higai placed paramount importance upon the acquisition of the Soul Channel's gift, but I think if he were here now, he would say the same as me. Before all else must come the defence of our land and our people.'

A man stepped up to Hanjo with a look of shock and barely disguised anger on his face. He was of slight build, clean-shaven, with neat hair tied back behind his head. Unlike those around him, he did not have the look of a hardened warrior.

'But, Hanjo, how can we trust...?'

'I trust them, Tomai, that should be enough for you, and for everyone else,' he cut in, turning to face his assembled men. 'I doubt any one of you would sleep easy with the thought that they may be telling the truth. The thought that any day now Kichibei's army could sweep through our land and destroy our homes and our families, while we sit here trying to harness a gift that was never meant to be ours. It is time to put aside vain self-interest and think of the innocent lives that could be lost if we do nothing. Now, if any of you still want to stay here, I will not try to stop you, but I would rather go to Harakima and discover they have lied than stay here and know forever after that I did nothing when a threat to my home was brought before me.'

Hanjo turned back to us without waiting to see how his speech had gone down.

'I take it you came here by boat,' Hanjo said to us.

'Well, we certainly didn't swim,' Kamari answered.

'Quite,' Hanjo replied, 'and your boat is waiting for you nearby?'

'It is,' I replied, before Kamari could make another insolent remark. 'A captain at Port Asukai volunteered to help us. He is waiting with the boat near the southern tip of the island.'

'Good. Please wait here, this will not take long,' Hanjo said. He turned back to his men and raised his arms for silence. 'My decision has been made – it is down to you now. Stand with me as you have always done and protect your homes and your families, or stay here and believe whatever you want to believe. Believe that this is not happening; believe that they are lying – whatever eases the shame that will consume your spirit when their story is proved true and our homeland is torn apart.'

Hanjo took a step nearer the men, studying the faces arrayed before him, a southerly wind whipping at his clothes.

'So, what do you say? Will you follow me once again, or will you stay?'

Murmurings broke out amongst the men once more as they all turned to look at each other, each waiting to see who would step forward and voice their answer first.

A tough-looking man emerged from the crowd. I recognised him as one of the guards who had been watching over Meera. He had been injured in the fight, fresh cuts on his face testament to this fact. He bowed to Hanjo, then turned to face the men and raised his sheathed sword above his head.

'Hanjo has never led us wrong before,' the man shouted to the assembled warriors. 'He has been a good and honest leader who has always done what is best for his men, his home and his lord. I say that, regardless of whether you believe these two,' here he gestured at Kamari and I, 'you believe in him, and follow him once more, wherever he may lead.'

Turning his back on his comrades the man moved to stand beside Hanjo.

'Thank you, Murai,' Hanjo said in an undertone to the man. Murai bowed but did not reply. As one, Hanjo's warriors moved to stand at his side, not one man choosing to disbelieve in him; in us.

'Then it is settled, we leave at once,' Hanjo called so all could hear. 'Murai, I'm putting you in charge of the men. Head back to camp and pack-up the important supplies. Leave the tents and anything else that would slow your return to Asukai. We will meet you there as soon as possible.'

'You are not coming with us?' Murai asked uncertainly.

'I will return with Wolf and Kamari and find out exactly what has been going on in Hirono during our absence,' Hanjo replied.

'As you wish,' Murai answered, bowing once more. Without another word, Hanjo turned and began to escort Kamari, Meera and I back to our boat.

Kamari and Hanjo were walking ahead of us between the trees, Kamari filling him in on everything that had occurred in Hirono over the past few months, from Zian Miyoshi and the battle at his fortress to this new threat from Shigako Kichibei. Several paces behind, I walked side by side with Meera, my mind abuzz. This was our first chance to speak alone and for a time I did not know what to say. My relief and love were so tangled-up with the hurt of her leaving me that in the end, all I managed was:

'I missed you…'

Meera looked up at me regretfully.

'I know, and I'm sorry… I missed you too, so very much,' she said, and I could feel the remorse emanating from her. 'But before we catch up, please tell me what is going on.'

I had so much more to say on this, but I knew she had not understood a word of what had been said earlier. I began by filling her in on the news about the imminent attack from Shigako Kichibei and the reason I had been sent to find her. I then related everything that had been said between myself, Kamari, Hanjo and his men. I could tell at once that not all of this news was completely new to her.

'I had felt something brewing in the east since before I was summoned to become the next Soul Channel,' she said, her voice inside my head uncurling much of the grief and anxiety that had lain bunched in my heart since she left me. 'I believe you felt it too, shortly before I… I left you…'

'I did,' I answered slowly, looking off into the trees ahead as we walked.

'So, the Council will not go to Orran's aid until I am safely back with them?' she asked after several minutes of quiet. I shook my head.

'Jaroe would have left for Harakima immediately, but without the full strength of the Council it would have been suicide,' I replied. 'Most of the Council believe the Kurai spirit is weak and unworthy of saving. They want to secure the Soul Channel and the continuance of their Council before they will march with us to Harakima; and they look to me and this task to prove the Kurai spirit still burns bright.'

Meera looked up at me then and I did not see the wolf but the woman whose spirit I had fallen in love with.

'I knew you would be the one to find me,' she said. 'It is what kept me going when Hanjo's men were examining me, when I was tied in that awful position and when… when the night closed in around me…'

I felt tears spring to my eyes as her voice echoed inside my head and the words I had wanted to speak to her since she had left finally escaped my lips.

'It has been so hard without you,' I said at last, stopping and looking down at her. 'Ever since you left I have felt like I'm drifting. I haven't slept, I've barely eaten and I have just felt like… like I'm coming apart, little by little each day – like waves eroding a cliff. And I have felt something drawing closer, an end of sorts, an inevitability I cannot escape.' Tears were falling down my face now as I looked at her. 'I need you, Meera; I need you more than you will ever know.'

She moved closer to me and I knelt down before her.

'All I want is to be with you, Takashi, my dear,' Meera replied, feelings of love, sadness, and grief at everything I had been through radiating from her. 'But we both know there is much to be done before then.'

I put my forehead against hers and felt peace flowing through me.

'When all this is over, we will be together, my love,' I whispered. 'One way or another, we will run together again.'

We were passing through the area of forest where the battle with the natives had taken place. I was walking side by side with Hanjo now and could see in his face the pity and remorse he felt. His head flicked here and there, taking in every detail of the scene around him, as though capturing it in his mind forever as punishment for what he had allowed to happen.

'We stumbled across them while out searching for food and fresh water,' he said to no one in particular. 'We did not notice the signs until it was too late, they attacked us first but… they were only defending their homes and their families.' Here he stopped speaking and knelt down by one of the corpses. Reaching towards its face, he closed its eyes. 'I should have been more careful, I should have sent scouts ahead, but instead we blundered through the forest like a pack of wild animals. This should not have happened…'

Neither of us knew what to say to comfort him. It was over now and no amount of remorse would undo it, so there was little we could say that would alleviate the pain he felt at walking through the scene of his mistake.

After what seemed like hours, I could once again hear the creak of rigging and the gentle slap of waves against wood that told us we had arrived.

'Takai!' I yelled as we reached the beach and began to wade to the ship. 'Make ready to sail!'

The captain appeared on deck and stopped still at the sight of us, his expression one of undisguised shock and amazement.

'What are… who are your companions?' he asked weakly.

'We'll explain once we've set sail,' Kamari said. 'We'll need some help getting Meera aboard.'

'Meera...?' he asked, still looking at us as though we were a figment of his imagination.

'Just help us,' I said hurriedly. Meera was swimming beside me and I could tell she was none too fond of the ocean. Her feelings of fear and anxiety washed over me, increasing in intensity as every wave lapped around her head.

It took three of us to hoist Meera on board the ship and by the end of it she was shaking and extremely upset. Kamari and Hanjo helped Takai make the ship ready to sail, with Kamari explaining all that had happened to Takai as they worked. I sat down by Meera in the prow of the ship and hugged her to my side, feeling her body quaking against mine.

'Don't worry,' I said comfortingly, smiling down at her. 'Getting off the ship will be much easier than it was to get on.'

The island was fast shrinking into the horizon, so small now that it appeared like a pebble being skipped across the vast expanse of the ocean. The journey back had begun in earnest. While everyone else was moving around the ship and drinking-in the life at sea, Meera had not moved since we had hauled her aboard. She had stood up several times to stretch her legs, but fatigue and the rocking of the ship soon sent her collapsing back to the deck. I had sat with her throughout the journey thus far, but she was clearly very uncomfortable and had said very little.

'I have developed a bitter dislike for sea voyages,' she said at last, after a long period of silence. 'I was transported here on board a ship in a small cramped box. The journey was not kind to me; it is something I will never forget.'

Here she paused and tried to stand, but sat back down again quickly. I looked furiously across at Hanjo who was at the wheel with Takai and Kamari, but found I could not bring myself to be angry with the man who had so readily agreed to help us.

'I don't think I'm cut out for a life at sea,' Meera said, with a valiant attempt at humour.

I laughed despite myself, despite the worry I felt at how badly this was affecting her. All I could think of was to try and keep her mind off the nauseating rocking of the ship.

'When you left to join the Council, did you have any idea what lay ahead of you?' I asked. 'Any idea of the importance of the path you were being drawn down?'

'No,' she answered. 'I had no idea what was to come. All I knew was I felt a force working on me; something inevitable, something irresistible, something I knew I could never escape from – just like you have felt yourself. There are greater forces at work in this world than simply man, Takashi.'

Those words stuck with me ever after. There are many people I have met in my life who would hate, deny or laugh at the thought that a path has been laid out before them; the thought that perhaps they are not in control of their lives and are instead following a predetermined route to a destination they cannot even guess at. But I say they are wrong. There is a path laid before all of us, but whether we choose to walk it and what we do along the way are up to the individual. Many stray from their path, whether consciously or unconsciously, but to do so is to risk missing the purpose – and maybe the reward – at the end of that path. And that is something I would not miss for anything.

At last Port Asukai appeared in the distance, drawing closer and closer as a strong easterly wind sped us onwards – as though the spirits themselves were aiding our journey. Wolf-grey clouds dominated the eastern skyline, boding rain to come. Such weather might have seemed like a bad omen, but I had a gut feeling that by the time we arrived at Harakima, the battle would have already begun, and heavy rain and fog would mask our approach on their rear.

'We're almost back at the port now, Meera,' I said, putting a comforting arm around her still-shaking body. 'We will soon be off this ship.'

She nodded in response, but did not say anything. Kamari had been throwing sly glances at me throughout the journey whenever he thought I wasn't looking. He was clearly concerned about both of us, but I could also tell how happy he was to see us back together at last.

He had left us alone until now, but at last approached us carrying two bowls in his hands. He knelt down in front of us and nodded awkwardly to Meera, clearly unsure how to behave around her.

'Thought you two could do with some food,' he said as bracingly as he could manage. 'We didn't bring much with us, but I was able to knock together this soup and I dug out some meat for Meera,' he added with a smile, placing the bowls down in front of us.

'I cannot bring myself to eat right now,' she said faintly. 'Once we are back on land, I will eat something, but please thank him for his kindness.'

'Meera is not feeling too well at the moment,' I said to Kamari, who nodded understandingly. 'But she would like to thank you for the kind thought.' Kamari nodded once more to Meera who returned the gesture. 'Thanks for the soup though,' I added, picking up my bowl and spoon and digging into the thin but adequate soup.

'No problem,' Kamari replied, standing up and moving back to the wheel to stand beside Takai.

A thought struck me then; a little insight into Kamari's mind. What must this be like for him? We had begun this journey together, but now I had found Meera again, it seemed possible – maybe even probable – that we would not end the journey together. I had sworn to Meera that we would be together one day; that we would run away together and if that happened… then I may never see him again. I knew he was happy we had found each other, but from the moment we realised what the Soul Channel actually was – when we realised it was Meera… he must have known that this would draw us apart once more, for – like all good friends – he knew my heart, and he knew I would follow her anywhere. We were like brothers, and I would always think of him as my brother, but my path seemed ever destined to follow in the wake of Meera's, and I would follow my path to its conclusion – whatever that may be.

I looked over at him, standing behind the wheel, steering the ship under Takai's watchful eye. We had been through so much together. I trusted him with my life and knew I could count on him in the battles to come, even if – when the dust settles – our paths diverge and I never see him again.

We were entering Asukai's harbour with the ship now being steered by the skilful Takai. Meera had at last managed to keep her feet and we now stood looking over the rail, watching the jetty come closer and closer. She was still extremely agitated and was twitching with impatience to get off the ship.

Finally, Takai halted the ship by the jetty and hardly had Kamari lowered the gangplank when Meera leapt off the ship to the solid stone of the harbour. Not far behind us, the rest of Hanjo's warriors – spread across five large ships – could be seen entering the harbour.

'There's no time to waste,' I said to Hanjo, Takai and Kamari as we strode down the gangplank. 'We must hasten to the Council of Wolves; once they see Meera is safe, they should help us defeat Kichibei.'

As we hurried to unpack the necessary supplies from Takai's ship, I found myself once more locked within my own mind. I tried to beat it down but it kept scratching its way to the surface – the one thought that had occupied me ever since it first needled its way into my brain – what would happen to Meera once we returned her to the Council? She was core to the Council's existence, the beating heart that bound them all together; they would be reluctant to *ever* let her put herself at risk. How could we be together under those circumstances?

Hanjo's men were speedily unloading their ships nearby as Kamari and I headed off into town to retrieve Dagri and our other supplies. However, we had barely set foot out of the harbour when I spotted several familiar faces moving through the crowded streets towards us.

'Oh no,' I whispered worriedly. 'I wondered if we'd be seeing them again…'

Kamari turned his head to watch as Tamoe and his friends approached us purposefully across the street.

CHAPTER THIRTEEN

Both Kamari and I instinctively reached for our weapons as Tamoe stopped in front of us, his hands held out in a gesture of friendship. I scanned both him and the men behind him, discerning no visible weapons. I did not, however, lower my guard.

'What do you want?' I asked, unable to keep the anger out of my voice.

'We mean you no harm,' Tamoe said, taking a step closer. 'On the contrary, we wish to apologise for our shameful behaviour when last we met. A life at sea is hard on a man's mind, body and spirit and that night we had all sought to drown our sorrows in drink. It seems we drowned ourselves a little too deeply.' A small smile appeared at his lips, but when we did not mirror it, he swiftly continued. 'What was said and done was fuelled by the alcohol in our veins, and I only wish we could take back our actions of that night.'

At his words I lessened the grip on my sword handle, affording me a sideways glance from Kamari who did not follow suit.

'Our deplorable actions brought shame on ourselves and our families,' Tamoe said bowing his head, the regret in his voice genuine. 'To alleviate this shame, we pledge ourselves to you, to aid you in whatever way you see fit.'

At a nod from Tamoe, he and his men bowed low before us. Looking a little startled, Kamari relaxed from his fighting stance and released the grip on his sword.

'You asked for aid that night and we shamefully rejected you,' Tamoe said from his bowed position. 'I only hope that we can still be of use to you somehow.'

'Stand up,' Kamari said to Tamoe and his men. 'When we tell you how you can help us, you may wish you had not made such an offer – the price may be too steep.'

'No price is too steep when a man's honour is on the line,' Tamoe replied, getting to his feet.

'On that we can agree,' Kamari said. 'If you are serious about helping us then we will gladly accept, but time is short. You, and as many men as you can round up, will accompany us into battle at Harakima – we will fill you in on the details on the way.'

It was testament to Tamoe's courage than he did not blanch at these words – his resolve did not even flicker.

'We will need horses,' I said to Tamoe. 'As many as you can find.'

'At once,' Tamoe said, hurrying off along the dock, his men trailing behind him.

Time seemed to have sped up, as though eager to chivvy us into battle. In the blink of an eye, several horses had been bought or borrowed and Tamoe had managed to round up almost one hundred men and boys – many of them sailors who had put to port that day – who would follow us into battle for Lord Orran.

Lack of sleep was weighing heavily upon me – punishing my aching, flagging body. The faces around me were blurred and indistinct as I peered at them through watery, bloodshot eyes. I did not know how much longer I could go on like this. I was so tired, but even with Meera back at my side, I could not sleep until the task Lord Orran had set me was complete and the end of my path revealed.

After saying goodbye to Takai and thanking him profusely for his help, I clambered into Dagri's saddle and looked down at Meera standing nearby. Again, the thought clawed its way into my brain, *what would happen when we brought her to the Council?* I needed her by my side – I could not bear to part from her so soon.

We had gathered as many supplies and weapons as we could find to sustain and arm us for the journey and battle ahead. Seated on horses at the head of our small army, Kamari, Hanjo, Tamoe and I – with Meera by my side – began to lead the way back to the wolves.

The journey back to the Council took considerably longer this time due to the task of keeping a small army of over two hundred people in check. But even though I knew it was taking longer than it should, it also seemed to take no time at all. Before we knew it, we had arrived on the outskirts of the forest where the wolves were holding Council.

The situation was delicate and as such required careful handling. We had joined forces with the men responsible for Meera's disappearance and I knew that if all was not explained, the wolves would tear Hanjo and his men apart. I ordered a halt to our march and explained the situation briefly to the people massed before me. My voice wavered slightly with the eyes of so many upon me, partly due to fatigue as well as nerves, but my words carried across the crowd so that even those at the back could hear.

When I had finished explaining, I told them to wait where they were while I spoke to the wolves. I turned from them and walked towards Kamari, Meera, Hanjo and Tamoe, who were standing to one side.

'They will not be happy to see you,' I said to Hanjo as I stopped beside him. 'In fact, once they know who you are, they will almost certainly try to kill you.'

'I am aware of this fact,' Hanjo said gravely, his voice steady, 'and I am prepared to accept the consequences of my actions. But I must be clear that I never condoned the task my lord set me. A lust for this gift had ensnared him and my protests were swept away by his greed. As you will understand, I was not able to disobey him, so I tried to fulfil his wishes in a way that did not bring me shame. I knew from the start that our task would be a failure, but I had to go through the motions to appease my lord.'

'I understand the predicament you were in,' I replied. 'I have seen such situations before.'

'If Hanjo is in such grave danger, would it not be best to leave him here while we go ahead and speak to the Council first?' Kamari asked.

'They would see that as just another insult,' I said. 'We must present Hanjo to them and explain the situation. Once they see that Meera has been returned safely and Hanjo has agreed to fight with us, it may stay their fury.'

I knelt down before Meera and stared into her face. She looked nervous and sorrowful and at once it made me feel so incredibly selfish. All this time I had thought solely about how difficult it would be for *me* to take her back to the Council, how difficult it would be for *me* if they were to separate us again. I had not spared a thought for how hard this all was for her. A great weight of responsibility and expectation had been thrust upon her; she was the Soul Channel, and although she was the force that bound the Council together, she was also separate from them. To them, she would always be something *other*, something detached – a prize to be protected, not a being to be close to. I realised it would be very lonely for her if – after the battles have been waged – they force her apart from me. I had not even asked how she felt about this; whether she saw it as a gift, or a curse...

'You know what is coming,' I said to her, barely able to speak the words.

'I know,' she replied. 'They will try to stop me going to battle with you and after… they may take me far away from you… they will not want to risk losing me again.'

I looked intently at her and felt a sudden madness grip me.

'We could run away now, you and I,' I whispered. 'We could run away and leave all this behind us.'

Even as I spoke the words, the madness left me and I knew that my honour would not allow me to do this. I felt ashamed for even thinking it.

'We must see this through to the end, my love,' she said quietly, 'and after, if we are meant to be together, for however brief a time, then it will be so.'

I buried my face in her fur, then stood quickly and led Kamari, Meera, Hanjo and Tamoe into the forest, towards the Council of Wolves.

The scene was exactly as I had left it, as though it were a moment frozen in time. The old quarry in the forest clearing, bathed in soft moonlight, illuminating rank upon rank of wolves arrayed along the rocky shelves. Innumerable stars gazed down upon us as we approached the Council – the wolves turning their heads at the sound of our footsteps.

As we reached the edge of the quarry, they parted to allow us access to the centre, all eyes now fixed upon Meera. Excited, relieved voices followed as we passed, but I could sense their suspicion at the two new men I had brought with me.

At last I reached the centre of the quarry and stood before Jaroe and Matai. I could feel their pleasure and their pride at seeing Meera returned, the feelings emanating so strongly, it was almost overwhelming. However, while Jaroe's attention was solely upon Meera, I could sense Matai's distrust of Hanjo.

'I knew you were the one to find her,' Jaroe said warmly, looking up at me. 'I sensed something about you the minute you set foot here. You have done what no wolf could do and you have proved the Kurai spirit is still alive – you have proved that there is hope for our Council yet.'

'Who are these men with you?' Matai asked quickly, unable to keep a low growl out of his voice.

'This man is called Tamoe,' I said pointing at him. 'He agreed to help us in the battle to come and has provided us with many...'

'Not him,' Matai cut across me. 'The other man. I sense something strange, something... disturbing about him.'

'His presence indeed needs explaining,' I said anxiously, 'but I must ask you to hear me out before you act.'

'I don't like this,' Matai said with a snarl. 'Who is this man you have brought to our Council? Speak quickly!'

'His name is Hanjo, he is a retainer of the southern lord, Higai...'

The result of these words was instantaneous. At once a great howling and snarling filled the air all around and the hackles on both Jaroe and Matai were raised. Matai's lips were drawn back over his jagged fangs as he leapt to his feet and made to spring at Hanjo, but I quickly placed myself between them. Not once did Hanjo flinch during all this.

'Please, please, you must listen to me!' I said frantically. 'Yes, it was Hanjo who organised the capture of Meera, but he was simply a soldier doing his lord's bidding – trapped between his duty and his own sense of what is morally right!' Matai took a step closer, a growl still rumbling deep in his throat. 'We all know what life is like, it is full of difficult choices, and sometimes we just have to do the best we can according to our own sense of honour and decency. I have spoken to Hanjo at great length and I know the position he was in was a difficult one. I too was dubious of him at first, but when I explained myself to him, explained why I was taking Meera back from him – when I was at his mercy and my life was in his hands – he put his faith in me. He believed in me when no other man in his position would have. He agreed to release Meera and come back to Harakima with his army to fight against Lord Kichibei for the freedom of Hirono. He won my trust there and then. You know I cannot lie to you, so I ask you to put aside your differences and stand by my side – as you promised you would – for Lord Orran.'

Matai did not back down, he was staring fixedly at Hanjo with a murderous look in his eyes. Jaroe's gaze was flicking between Hanjo and Matai until he seemed to come to a decision. He walked forward, placing himself between the wolf and the man, his eyes remaining on Hanjo. Then he turned to face Matai.

'Brother… what Hanjo did was unforgivable. Taking Meera from us is something he will never be able to redeem himself of. But what he did after is enough to earn our trust. We cannot undo the deeds of the past, but we can learn from them, and in some ways… we can change. I believe Takashi and… I believe that Hanjo wishes to help us.'

Matai did not say anything but instead his growl deepened and his muscles visibly flexed.

'I need you to stand by me, brother,' Jaroe said to Matai, lowering his voice slightly. 'Takashi has fulfilled his side of our agreement, he has brought Meera back to us and he has proved there is spirit left in the Kurai worth fighting for. Many of the Council look to you, and not to me, for leadership. I need you to stand by me now so we may bring them together to fight for Lord Orran once again.'

Matai's growl slowly ceased and his gaze at last turned to meet Jaroe's. He moved back slightly and sat down.

'I do not like this arrangement, but I will put aside my mistrust for you, brother,' Matai said in a low voice. 'You are right, Takashi has fulfilled his side of the agreement admirably. Lord Orran will have our full support in the battle to come – the Council will go to his aid once more.'

Jaroe nodded his thanks to his brother then turned back to face us.

'Now that is settled, we have one more thing to attend to before we march,' Jaroe said, his eyes now falling upon Meera who had sat quietly throughout. He beckoned her closer with a flick of his muzzle and she obeyed. 'Meera, words cannot express how glad we are to see you amongst us again. I hope you are alright after everything you have been through?'

'I am fine,' she said tiredly, glancing across at me and holding my gaze for a moment. 'Hanjo made sure no hurt came to me.'

A strange expression crossed Jaroe's face when he noticed the look that passed between Meera and I. But it was gone in a second, leaving me unsure I had even seen it. Had he sensed the feelings we held for each other? And if he had, would he do anything about it?

'Good, I am glad to hear that,' he said warmly. Turning to the wolves massed around the quarry, Jaroe spoke loudly and clearly. 'The Soul Channel has been returned to us – Takashi has brought Meera home!'

A great howling rent the air as every wolf present pointed their muzzle to the night sky and howled their pleasure to the stars. But I could not join them in their elation. Jaroe's use of the word "home" made me realise how futile my love for Meera was. The Council would never allow her to leave with me. This could be the last time I ever see her…

'Meera is returned to us!' Matai howled over the voices of those around him. 'We leave for Harakima immediately! Orran will have our help one last time, so let us make this a battle that will never be forgotten!'

With one last long, unified howl, the wolves turned as one and began to clamber to the top of the quarry, massing at the edge of the clearing to await their leaders.

Jaroe nodded to two wolves at the back of the crowd and they walked over, feelings of fierce pleasure and lust for battle radiating from them. Meera bowed her head sorrowfully. She knew what this meant and so did I.

'Brothers,' Jaroe began, once the two wolves were standing at our sides. 'To you I entrust the most important task of all.'

The body language of the two wolves was enough to betray their feelings. Their shoulders drooped, it was clear they knew what was coming too.

'We cannot risk losing Meera again,' he said sternly. 'It would be the greatest blow this Council has ever suffered. To get her back only to lose her in the coming battle? I will not let it happen. You must guard her and keep her safe from any who would do her harm.'

Here his voice softened and he moved closer to the two wolves, whose heads were bowed dejectedly.

'I know you want nothing more than to enter battle, but I would not have appointed you if I did not trust you most of all,' Jaroe continued seriously. 'You may take her to a safe viewing distance, but you must not allow her to put herself in harm's way.'

The two wolves nodded and stepped respectfully to one side. Jaroe turned to Meera and looked at her kindly.

'I can see into your heart, Meera, and I know you want to follow us into battle… for many reasons,' Jaroe said, glancing at me in a way that confirmed my earlier suspicions. 'But I don't think you realise just how important you are. You must not put yourself at risk. Not for anything. Promise me this.'

'I will do whatever is necessary to reach the end of my path,' she said mysteriously.

Jaroe looked as though he was going to say something, but with one last glance between myself and Meera, he seemed to decide against it. Matai stepped in for Jaroe who had gone strangely quiet.

'You two know your job,' he said to the two wolves, who nodded in acknowledgment. 'Perform it to the best of your abilities. Now, we must move – Kichibei may have already begun his attack on Harakima.'

I nodded to Kamari, indicating that all was well and he should head back to join the rest of the army. He nodded back and set off through the trees with Tamoe and Hanjo. As everyone else began to move off to join the other wolves, I knelt down before Meera and touched my forehead gently to hers.

'I will not say goodbye because this is not the last I will see you,' I said, feeling the first prickle of tears soon to fall. 'To hell with the consequences. I don't care what we have to do, I don't care where we have to run, I don't care who I have to kill, I don't…' I felt my body begin to shudder uncontrollably. 'I know we are meant to be together, I know that our paths will one day join.'

'If you truly believe that, my love,' Meera said tenderly. 'Then it will be so.'

I turned then and walked away from her, leaving her seated with her two wolf guards, but looking more isolated than I had ever seen her.

CHAPTER FOURTEEN

Kamari held Dagri steady as I mounted up beside him, my eyes trained on the east – on the place where Harakima lay. He did not say anything, but simply having him beside me made it less difficult to walk away from her.

Just as it was when I returned to Aigano with my mind full of my father's murder, I knew that the only way I could go on was to force her from my thoughts. I knew that if I did not, I would be unable to continue. Thankfully, there was something else ready and waiting to occupy my mind – I still had to find out what Kamari had been keeping from me ever since we left Aigano...

Our small army of southern men and dock workers were much less surprised to see me emerge from the trees at the head of an army of wolves than I had expected. I had explained everything to them in brief before entering the woods, but I had still expected their appearance to be greeted by shock, or even fear. But clearly most people here had heard the legends surrounding the wolves and so were not taken aback to see them line up before them, rank after rank of lean, grey-haired bodies.

Everyone knew how little time we had. There was no time for great speeches to spur the troops into battle, no time to raise their spirits before the combat to come. At the head of this army of wolves and men I raised my sword and pointed it towards Harakima, signalling the march to begin – the final stretch of the journey.

Or so I thought…

There was very little talk as the hours slipped by and we drew ever closer to Harakima. I had spent the time, not thinking about the battle ahead, but thinking about how I could get Kamari to tell me the secret I felt – or rather I *knew* – he wanted to tell me. In the end I realised I had nothing – no way to force him to open-up that would not shame me. We were riding into battle and possibly our deaths; I could not travel by his side without first knowing what it was he was so reluctant to tell me. I just had to ask him one last time…

'Kamari…' I began, struggling to think how best to phrase this final request.

'I know what you're going to ask… you are transparent, my friend,' Kamari said, with the ghost of a smile. 'In truth, I have been thinking about nothing else since we set out.'

'Then just tell me!' I said earnestly, turning in the saddle to meet his gaze. 'Tell me what you have been hiding from me ever since we left Aigano. I know you feel you should tell me, so just say it!'

Kamari let out a deep sigh and ran his hands agitatedly through his hair. He looked torn – unsure whether to show allegiance to his friend or whoever he was protecting.

'It is difficult,' he said at last. 'I find myself trapped between my honour and my friend. Whichever I choose, I will feel shamed… I either have to break my word or risk losing your trust and your friendship.'

'Are we not brothers?' I said, leaning closer to him. 'You ride into battle at my side – there must be no secrets between us. Tell me what you have been hiding!'

'Your mother is dying!'

Kamari blurted it out so fast that I was caught completely off guard. My head reeled and I had to grip Dagri's saddle to prevent myself falling to the brittle grass below. Right then, everything crystallised into a whole I could finally make sense of. I had thought at the time that my mother had been acting strangely, but my mind had been so caught up in the task ahead, I had not registered its significance. She had seemed frail and wan, which I had put down to the shock of my arrival. I recalled the moment I entered our home when she made a move to stand and embrace me, but had instead waited for me to come to her. And when I called the town meeting she had opted to stay home, saying she already knew what was happening, but really she had been too ill to move. She had been hiding her illness from me, and it seemed Kamari had too.

'Why didn't you tell me?!' I screamed in Kamari's face, reining Dagri to a halt and forcing our army to flow around us like water around rock.

'She made me promise not to, she believes it is her time to die! She believes it so strongly in her heart that nothing should be done to stop it!'

'My mother is dying and you do not think something should be done to prevent it!' I yelled at him, hardly able to comprehend how I had ever called him brother. 'I have to go to Aigano now, I… I have to talk to her!'

'This is exactly why she did not want you to know,' Kamari said, trying to reason with me. 'She knew you would go haring off to try and stop it, regardless of the consequences and regardless of her own wishes!'

But I was barely listening to him; my mind was a whirlwind of emotion as I tried to rationalise it all in my head.

'How could she sit there and not fight her own death! What about Mia? What was to happen to her? Has she forgotten her own daughter?' The words tumbled out of my mouth, sounding hysterical to my ears.

'Ellia and I agreed to care for Mia after… after she… You must understand we were simply following her wishes and what she made most clear was that she did not want you to try and prevent this!'

'Oh, so you even planned what was to happen after her death!' I spat viciously, glaring at my supposed friend. I turned away from him, unable to look at him a second longer.

'If she is as ill as you say then she would not have left Aigano with the others.'

I turned Dagri northwards and he reared up on his hind legs at the sudden tug on the reins.

'Lead the army to Harakima,' I said to Kamari without looking at him. 'I will join you there soon. You see, I know what it means to be brothers…'

Lashing Dagri hard with the reins, I spurred him on northwards.

'I'm sorry! You must believe me, I was only respecting your mother's wishes!' Kamari yelled after me, his voice breaking with emotion.

Dagri was snorting with exertion as I forced him onwards, faster than I had ever driven him before. His flanks heaved mightily as he sucked in great gulps of air to fuel his flagging limbs. It was frighteningly dark between the trees, for I was now deep within Shizuka Forest, taking the most direct route back home. Branches raked my face and neck and I felt blood sliding down my cheeks and into my eyes and mouth, but I did not try to avoid them. If anything, I welcomed them – how could I have been so stupid? How could I not have seen it?

In my sleep-addled mind I recalled the last thing my mother had said to me before I left Aigano:

'We each follow our own paths; our own instincts and beliefs. I know yours will lead you right.'

I now knew what she had meant. She had told me this so I would understand later. She was dying; that was her belief and her instincts were telling her that she had reached the end of her path and it was time to give up fighting. But she had too much left to fight for to simply give up. I just had to get there and make her understand that before it was too late.

All else had been blotted out of my mind in the instant Kamari told me the truth. Meera, Harakima, Lord Orran, Kichibei; these things all seemed strangely insignificant to me now. This – right now – was more important than anything in the world and everything else would have to wait until it had been dealt with. I could not lose her. When it hit me – truly hit me – that she might die, I knew I could not go on without her. I could not go on without knowing that she was there in Aigano, always available for me to turn to. She was my constant. I needed her. Mia needed her. I could not sit back and let this happen.

But how much longer could I go on like this? My body was screaming at me to stop and rest, but I could not afford to listen to it yet. I had not slept for days now – weeks probably. I couldn't even remember the last time I had slept more than a few minutes. I could barely concentrate anymore, could hardly see. My body could only take so much and it seemed it had almost reached its limit. Not much further, I kept telling myself, not much further…

I tasted earth, leaves and blood as I slipped from the saddle and thudded to the muddy forest floor, sliding to a stop at the base of a tree, my sword handles digging painfully into my side. For a moment I could not move – did not want to move – my racing heartbeat matching the sound of Dagri's hooves as he cantered to a stop. My fingernails raked the earth as I tried to haul myself up, but my arms were shaking so badly I could not manage it. I rolled onto my back and lay there, bloody, bruised and exhausted.

Dagri trotted over and began to nudge me with his nose, as if he too knew the urgency of the situation. I had to get up and continue, no matter how painful it was, I had to keep going. But it would be so easy to just lie here and forget about everything – forget about all my troubles and rest. The temptation was great and I felt the minutes stretch out before me as I lay there unmoving.

No. Now was not the time to rest. I had much left to do and very little time to do it in. Rest could come later, or it could not come at all. Dagri's reins were dangling near my head and slowly, painfully, I reached up and grabbed them. As I did so Dagri began to move backwards, hauling me to my feet. My legs shook badly with every step I took, but I soon managed to clamber into his saddle. I leaned in close to his ear and stroked his neck.

'Thank you, my friend,' I whispered.

With an encouraging lash of the reins, Dagri broke into a canter and we continued on to Aigano.

CHAPTER FIFTEEN

It was early morning by the time we came in sight of Aigano. Dagri seemed to know we were near our destination, for he put on a burst of speed I would not have thought possible. Galloping full-tilt along the western bank of the Kohaku River, I wondered whether I would be too late. How badly ill had she been when last I saw her? Only she knew that, but soon, so would I.

A cold wind whipped my face as we flew along, the first rays of the sun reflecting brightly off the river at my side, turning it into a path of white light leading me home.

I could see the house now. The house where I grew up, where I assumed she now sat. I realised I could be way-off in my guess; perhaps she *had* gone to Harakima with the others and coming here was just more time wasted. But if I knew her like I thought I knew her, she would not want to die anywhere other than the village she grew up in. But then, she had hidden her illness from me… so perhaps I did not know her as well as I thought…

I reined Dagri to a halt outside the house and leapt from the saddle, running like a man possessed towards the door and sliding it open with such force that it broke and fell to the floor with a clatter. Breathing hard, I rushed down the corridor and into the main room and saw her.

She was seated in the exact same place I had last seen her, her body in the posture of one at prayer. Her skin was extremely pale and she looked painfully thin. I thought for a moment she was already dead, then her eyes opened and she looked blearily up at me.

'Why didn't you tell me!?' I cried, hurrying over and kneeling before her. She sighed and looked past me, out of the open window.

'Because I knew you would not understand,' she said, her voice as frail as she looked.

'You're right, I do not understand! Why would you not fight your own death? Why would you not strive to live for the sake of your friends, for your daughter, for... for me...?' I said, my voice trailing off as I looked at her.

She sighed again and beckoned me to her, coughing painfully as I moved to sit by her side.

'When I was younger, I remember saying the same thing to my mother. I remember asking her why she did not seek healing. She told me that when it is your time to die you... you just know it... You feel it deep inside,' she said, clutching her breast as she looked into my face and saw the first tears begin to fall.

'You cannot feel that now! You do not feel that now!' I said, anger clouding my grief. 'What your mother said has misled you! It is not your time to die and that is something I feel deep inside me!'

'Takashi… this feeling within me is real, I cannot ignore it… it is my time.'

'You can't die!' I heard myself screaming, viewing myself from outside as though my consciousness had slipped from my body. 'You are one of the few constants in my life! I need you here! Mia needs you here! She cannot grow up so young without a mother and father! Forget your instincts, forget your feelings, not always do they lead you right! Think about your children; you must live on; you must live on for us!'

I was breathing heavily and felt light-headed, as though I might collapse at any minute. My mother was staring at me and tears now ran freely down her cheeks.

'There is a healer known to live deep in the Mahari Forest northeast of our valley,' she said, pointing out of the window. 'If you can find him and bring him back here, then yes… he may be able to heal me. But Takashi, you must understand that all my life, I have been led to believe that when you feel it is your time, then… then your path has reached its end… Of course, I want to live, of course I want to stay and watch my beautiful children grow up! But it is a belief that has been deeply ingrained in me, a belief passed down by my ancestors for generations. I fear that, even if you were to bring back the healer, it would be too late!'

'It won't be too late!' I said stubbornly. 'I will be back as soon as I can. You have not reached the end of your path yet – I will prove it to you!'

With one final look at her, I leapt to my feet and ran out of the house and down the steps. Dashing tears from my eyes, I jumped into Dagri's saddle and spurred him swiftly northwards. Within seconds we had crossed the bridge that spanned the river and continued north along the eastern bank, passing through the village that now appeared like a ghost town. Memories flooded in on me as I rode, but as with every other thought currently fighting for control of my mind, I simply forced myself not to think about them.

So… a healer somewhere in the Mahari Forest…? My mother's description did not inspire me with confidence, but somehow I knew that I would find him, one way or another. It was midday and the forest was finally in sight. The sun rode high in the sky and the day had turned out to be brilliantly clear, the weather a perfect juxtaposition to my frantic and anxious mood.

With my sights trained on the forest, it was a while before I noticed the approach of several men on horseback. At first mere specks on the horizon, it soon became clear that they were riding in the direction of Aigano. With my suspicions aroused, I reined Dagri to a halt and turned, watching them draw closer. There were five of them, each garbed in strange armour

I had never seen before and bearing crests I did not recognise. My blood ran cold. I knew who had sent these men and I knew why they were here.

I guided Dagri back along the path we had just ridden, seeking to intersect the course of the five men heading for my home. But I need not have bothered. They had already turned and were heading in my direction. I had nowhere to turn, nowhere to stand that would give me the high-ground in the coming fight – for the vast grassy plains stretched away in every direction. There was not even a rock or tree in sight to put my back against. I dismounted Dagri and let his reins fall loose. With my arms held out soothingly, I backed away, indicating that he should stay where he was. When I was far enough away and satisfied that Dagri would not get hurt in the coming fight, I turned to face the approaching men.

I watched them fan out as they drew near and detected their arrogance immediately. The way they held themselves, the way they looked down their noses at me – to them I held no more significance than an insect. I felt fury building within me as I watched cruel smiles spread across their faces at the thought of the slaughter to come.

Without a word they encircled me, but I did not draw my weapons. I simply stood there calmly, as though I had submitted to the inevitable. I could feel the fury gripping me tighter and tighter, slowly working its way throughout my being, taking control of body and mind.

'What have we here?' one of the men said, the sneer in his voice feeding my rage.

'Must be one of the brats from Aigano,' a second man said, laughing harshly.

'You're a long way from home, little boy,' another said, leaning in close to me.

'It's like he knew we were coming,' the first man said, reaching out a foot to prod me in the back. 'Were you trying to run from the slaughter? Did you think you could escape Lord Kichibei?'

'You cannot escape him, young one,' the second man said. 'Harakima will fall and then Aigano and Toramo, and once we have taken Hirono, the south will follow – even that fool Higai's province will bow to us. You have nowhere to run.'

'It seems he has been struck dumb, Malai!' one of the men joked with their leader.

'I have that effect on people,' he said maliciously. 'Particularly on young upstarts who think they are warriors.'

As he said this, he kicked the twin swords that hung at my side.

'Have you nothing to say for yourself, little fool?' the second man said. 'No last words?'

He leaned in towards me and spat at my feet, his face twisted with malice and hatred. As he did so I felt the fury swell and uncurl within me. I could not have fought it even if I had wanted to. The only other time I had felt like this had been at Zian's fortress, just after Meera died. Kamari had told me that in that moment I had looked more like a wolf than a man, and now I felt that same intoxicating power reach crescendo. As it did so, I felt the now familiar feeling of inevitability pulsing inside me. The two were intrinsically linked, but I did not yet know what they meant. But in that moment, I did not care. Like a moth into the flame, I was drawn towards it… and surrendered to them completely.

With a growl that can only be described as wolf-like, I hauled the man who had spat at me from his horse and hurled him to the ground. I had slid my sword from its sheath and driven it through his neck into the grass before any of the others had even registered what had happened. With furious, anguished yells, the four remaining men scrabbled at their sword hilts, fumbling in their haste. I wrenched my sword free of the dead man and – hefting it like a spear – threw it at the one I took to be their leader. The sword pierced his armour and drove straight through his heart. With a look of complete shock and confusion, he weakly tugged at the sword handle protruding from his chest before his body went limp, and he toppled from his horse. Hastily, I drew my other sword and snatched a second from the dead man lying at my feet.

The next few minutes are a blur on my memory. My two swords moved as though they had lives of their own, cutting through horse and man alike. I am not proud of it. If I had had any semblance of control over myself, I would not have injured those animals; but I do not pretend that I had any say in my actions. I had given up control – and given it willingly – and this was the price to be paid. Screams and terrified neighing filled the air, but I heard it all as though from a great distance away.

What I remember most clearly was a pair of wolf eyes. They hung before my vision – ethereal and wispy – gifting me briefly with the sight and senses of a wolf. They were senses I now realised I had tapped into before, on my journey to the Council and to rescue Meera. It frightened and intrigued me and it was some time before I realised that all movement around me had ceased. Silence had descended across the plains – all sound vanishing as suddenly as snuffing out a candle. The eyes faded from my vision and I was left in the midst of the carnage I had wrought.

Bewildered and shaking, I stumbled towards the leader and pulled my sword from his chest. With my eyes wide and staring, I wiped my swords on the grass and walked slowly back to Dagri. I gripped his reins feebly and clambered into the saddle. Nudging my heels into his flanks, I urged him on, away from a scene I would never be able to forget.

We had not been riding long when we reached the edge of the forest. From the outside it appeared calm and tranquil, but I had come to distrust the silence found deep between trees, for I had learned that it often hid hatred, malice and hunger. As slowly and quietly as possible, I dismounted and led Dagri between the trees – careful to avoid all branches in my path so as not to disturb birds or other forest creatures.

I did not know how I was going to locate this healer, for he could be anywhere in this vast expanse of woodland – or he could be nowhere… Something told me, however, that I would not need to find him – that he would find me, and choose to reveal himself or not.

I was soon so deep in the forest I could no longer see the plains between the trees and thus far had seen nothing that indicated a person lived here; no signs of footprints or fires, no traps or snares – nothing. It was as I rounded a particularly large and gnarled beech tree that a strange construction greeted my eyes. A ramshackle hut made of wood, leaves and mud stood at the foot of a tree in a small clearing, looking for all the world as though it had been abandoned for years. Cobwebs and bird droppings covered the roof and walls, and insects scuttled in and around it. I led Dagri cautiously towards it and stopped outside what I took to be the front door. With a sinking feeling in my stomach, I let go of Dagri's reins and took a step closer.

'Hello?' I called out, my voice instantly swallowed up by the encroaching trees.

There was no answer, but above me a bird cawed harshly and took flight. I took another step towards the door and knocked gently upon it. After receiving no response, I pushed the door open and poked my head in. What I saw inside surprised me greatly, given the appearance of the outside. The room within was small but extremely clean and tidy. A table and chair stood against one wall, a rough cabinet filled with bottles and jars stood against another and books and scrolls were stacked in one corner. I was just about to take a step into the room when a voice called out behind me.

'Are you a friend?' the voice said, loudly but not angrily.

I whipped around and scanned the surrounding trees. It was a male voice and sounded raspy, as though the speaker was very old. For a minute I was lost for words, my first thought being to draw my sword.

'Excuse me?' I said at last, crouching low and looking everywhere for signs of a threat.

'It's just that, you invited yourself into my home, so I assume you must know me very well,' the voice continued, a hint of annoyance now discernible.

'I'm sorry that I intruded,' I said, standing up straight once more. 'I came here to seek the aid of a healer to...'

'Your mother is ill and you wish me to look at her,' he said inconceivably, as though he had read my mind.

'Yes, but...'

'It is not her that asks for the healing, it is you.'

'My mother is confused; her thoughts have been twisted by tales her family told her. She believes it is her time to die and so is not fighting it. But how can that be? She has two children that need her, one still so young that the loss of her mother could destroy her. How can it be her time to die?' I asked, barely managing to keep a sob out of my voice.

'So, you believe you know better than your mother when it is her time to die?'

Stubbornly, I took a step closer to the voice.

'I do not believe the spirits would take her away from me… from Mia and I so soon,' I replied adamantly. 'We have already lost our father, I do not think the spirits would be so cruel as to take her from us as well.'

'I would have thought by now you would have realised that life is not always a pleasant ride. Have you ever thought that maybe she wishes to die?' the strange voice asked, pinpointing a fear I had held ever since speaking to my mother. 'That maybe she wants to join her husband in the next life?'

'No!' I replied at once, sounding far more confident than I felt. 'She told me she wants nothing more than to live on and watch the two of us grow up, but that the feeling within her was too strong to ignore. I persuaded her that her feeling is false, that there is too much left for her to live for!'

'And you believe that? Truly believe that?'

'I do,' I said, all shred of doubt finally gone.

As those words faded into the forest, a figure stepped out from behind a tree and strode quickly towards me. He was small and elderly, his long white hair tied in a knot at the back of his head. He had a short, neat beard and appeared strong and able-bodied for his age. He wore a three-quarter length kimono that had once been deepest blue but had long since faded. In his right hand he clutched a curiously bulging cloth bag and the way he held it to his chest made it clear it was precious to him.

'Then I will come back with you and care for your mother,' the man said. 'My name is… or was, a long time ago, Ikushima Terai.'

'Takashi Asano,' I said, bowing low before him in thanks.

Dagri barely seemed to notice the extra weight as Ikushima and I rode back to Aigano, bearing the two of us as if we weighed no more than children. We had delayed only a couple of minutes as Ikushima gathered a few things from his house, then I had gripped his hand and hauled him onto Dagri behind me.

And now we rode fast and straight towards Aigano, the wind whipping our hair and faces and billowing our clothes out around us. Dagri's hooves pounded the soft grass, speeding us on towards the spot where I had taken five men's lives. My throat grew tight as we drew ever closer and I wondered if Ikushima would know what had happened and who was responsible. I guessed that he would, for he had already proven himself a strangely perceptive man.

The scene was worse than I remembered as we rode swiftly past. Dark crimson blood stained the grass all around, pooling here and there. Crows and other scavenging birds were walking over the bodies, pecking at the eyes and faces of the dead men. It was a sight so gruesome I could not look at it for more than a few seconds. Ikushima, however, stared unblinkingly at the bodies, his eyes never leaving them as we rode away. He did not say anything, but I sensed that something had changed between us. What that was I would never find out – whether his respect for me had been heightened, or his disgust of me intensified – I would never know.

The afternoon was drawing swiftly on and darkness would soon be here. I was running out of time. I had to return to Aigano before continuing on to Harakima, where the battle may have already been joined. I wearily rubbed my eyes and noticed that my hands were stained with blood. Hoping Ikushima hadn't noticed, I surreptitiously wiped them on my haori and gripped the reins tighter. The stain was still there, but I paid it no mind. My hands were only going to get bloodier in the hours to come.

My legs were aching after sitting in the saddle for so long. I had been riding almost constantly since we left Asukai and this – combined with my general aches, pains and tiredness – left me wondering how long it would be before I collapsed again. But thinking this, I suddenly realised how silly it was to complain about my legs aching when Dagri was carrying two men on his back.

The sun was low on the western horizon by the time we thundered into Aigano. Poor Dagri was snorting with tiredness and his legs were shaking with fatigue as I walked him across the bridge and dismounted outside my house. I helped Ikushima from his back, then led Dagri swiftly down the bank where he could drink from the cold, fast-flowing river.

Ikushima had already gone inside the house, so I hurried quickly after him. By the time I got into the main room, he was already kneeling before my mother and speaking softly to her. He reached into his cloth bag and drew out several incense burners. He lit these from one of the nearby candles and soon a soothing, cleansing smell filled the air around us.

I was hovering in the doorway, knowing in my heart I had to leave immediately, but unwilling to abandon my mother. She looked so peaceful sitting there, I almost could not tell she was ill. Then I realised it was a calmness brought on by acceptance. She did not think the healer would be able to help her and was prepared for the inevitable. I bit my lip with anxiety and it was several seconds before I noticed that blood was dripping down my chin. I hastily wiped the blood on the back of my hand and was about to take a step into the room, when:

'You have somewhere else to be, yes?' Ikushima asked me, his uncanny senses scaring me once again.

'Yes, I do but…'

'There is nothing more you can do for me, Takashi,' my mother said, smiling kindly at me. 'Either

Ikushima will heal me, or he will not. Standing there watching will not help in any way. You have so many important things left to do and you still have your whole life ahead of you, to live how you see fit with whoever you choose to live with. You said I was one of the few constants in your life, but Takashi, my dear, whatever should happen, you know I will always be here for you. I will always be watching over you, always here to listen to your hopes and worries… and I will *always* love you, my son.'

Crying openly, I walked towards her and knelt down to hug her thin body to me. Her eyes were dry when she looked at me, gripping me by the shoulders and holding me at arm's length.

'You have made me so proud, my brave Takashi,' she said. 'Now go, and please do not worry about me – life is complicated enough without adding worry to it.'

I kissed her on the forehead and without a word, stood and left the room.

Dagri stood where I had left him by the river. His legs were no longer shaking but still, instead of riding him, I gripped him by the reins and led him at a slow pace across the bridge onto the eastern bank. I wiped at my eyes, which were blurred by tears, and looked back at the house. That house was the one place I had always felt safe and secure and if… if… I could not even bring myself to say it… *If* the worst happened, I would have nowhere left; nowhere to go when I felt alone or scared, nowhere but an empty house full of grief and ghosts.

No. That was not true. It would not just be a house of ghosts. That house was a direct link to my mother and father, regardless of what happened. Memories of a happier past would always be alive there and no matter what the future held, those memories would give me the strength I needed when times were hard. So, whatever happened, there would be a constant in my life – and that was a comforting thought indeed.

I climbed into Dagri's saddle and – without looking back – rode off south through the valley on my way back to Harakima castle, and the end of my path.

CHAPTER SIXTEEN

It was fast approaching the spirit hour and so far I had neither seen nor heard anything of Harakima. It was so dark I could not even see Dagri beneath me, leaving me with the strange sensation of floating through the air. Trees and rocks stood out eerily against the lighter grey of the horizon as we whipped past them at breakneck speed. I knew that riding this fast in the dark was dangerous, that we could easily be killed if Dagri were to step in a hole or trip on a rock, but I did not dare slow down. The army Kamari and I had assembled would be a good way ahead of me by now, and chances were they had already joined the battle.

Thinking on what lay ahead, my thoughts flew to Kamari and everything I had said to him when we parted. I felt deeply ashamed of my harsh words and wondered what had possessed me to say them. I had encountered Kamari's situation before and knew how hard it could be to decide on the right thing to do. He had been trapped between his word of honour to my mother and his loyalty to me. I can only imagine the terrible pressure he must have endured to keep this secret for so long. And what had I done when he finally made his decision and chose me over his word? I had reprimanded him instead of thanking him for his loyalty. I wondered whether he would ever forgive me for what I said, or whether he would even be alive to apologise to, when I reached Harakima...

Distantly, I heard the first sounds of combat ringing across the plains. Screams, snarls and the clashing of steel echoed off the walls of the castle and carried on the breeze towards me. My detour had cost me dearly. The surprise attack on Kichibei's forces had already been launched, and I had not been there to lead it. A howl rent the air, the proud and ferocious call of a wolf revelling in the slaughter of his enemies. I knew who it was at once - Matai.

At first, I had distrusted Matai and felt righteous disdain for the way he had split the Council when we needed their help. But now I knew the reasons for it. Now I knew how important the Soul Channel was to them. So many times before, they had been forced to drop everything and jump to the Kurai's aid, leaving their own problems by the wayside. This time their own problem had simply been too great to ignore. Matai had merely been looking out for the Council, for his brothers and sisters. Now I knew the full story, it was not so unreasonable, but it made my future with Meera seem all but impossible...

The castle was finally in view. It sat like a beacon on the lower slopes of the Eastern Mountains that split the domain from north to south, the blazing torches that lined the walls illuminating a scene of carnage on the plains below. Our army of wolves and men had attacked from the west – hitting the rear of Kichibei's army – and were now cutting a swathe through them towards the main gate of the castle.

From this distance I could see Kurai archers on the wall-tops firing flaming arrows upon Kichibei's warriors, who were engaged in attacking the main gate with a battering ram, adding a dull staccato rhythm to the combat. As I neared the rear of the battle, I could see the gate had already taken extensive damage. Cracks could be discerned running up and down the once sturdy door and the enemy yelled war cries with every crash of the ram upon the buckling wood.

I drew my sword from its sheath as I neared the back of our army, who were pushing valiantly through Kichibei's forces. Blurs of grey fur spattered with crimson leapt here and there, tearing flesh from bones and ripping limbs from bodies as easily as cutting heads off flowers. And just like that, I was in the thick of it.

Drawing alongside the wolves, I brought my sword into play on a man poised to throw a spear at a wolf. My blade tip found his throat and sliced it open, spurting blood over Dagri's flank.

To my immense pride and gratitude, the horse did not even flinch at the chaos all around us. He had grown and matured a lot in the time I had known him. I remembered the first time I saw him; a fine, strong-looking animal, but terribly nervous with it, starting at the slightest noises. Now, here he was, riding into battle like a true war horse – no fear, no quarter, his eyes set only on the goal – the gate.

I lashed out with my blade at foes on either side, scanning the melee desperately for signs of Kamari. But with only moon and torchlight, it was difficult to even separate enemies from comrades. Instead, I headed for our vanguard, who were on the verge of breaking through Kichibei's forces to the main gate. An arrow whipped by my arm and I almost lost my grip on the reins. Scrabbling frantically at the saddle, I just managed to cling on and right myself. A second arrow thudded into Dagri's shoulder and he whinnied in pain and shock, but did not stop his headlong charge as blood flowed freely from the wound. Praying that it wasn't barbed, I reached down in the saddle and gently pulled it out. Dagri did not even grunt as the arrow was removed, did not slow his pace at all. I was prouder of him now than I had ever been.

Just up ahead I spotted the archer responsible. He was notching another arrow to his bowstring and beginning to take aim once more. The next arrow whistled between Dagri's legs and I realised he had been aiming for him from the start. With an enraged yell I raised my sword as the archer fumbled for another arrow. The blade cut the bow in two and opened up a gaping hole in the man's chest, exposing his ribcage. Without a sound, the archer crumpled to the floor – never to rise.

I rode on; snarling, growling wolves on my left and screaming, shouting men on my right – my ears ringing with the sounds of death all around. *Was Kamari alright?* The thought throbbed through my brain as I slashed here and there, shame gnawing at my heart. I would never forgive myself if he died before I could apologise to him.

At last I spotted him. He was at the forefront of the wolf army, fighting side by side with Jaroe and Matai. I had changed course and was heading for him – desperate to reach his side – when a huge figure, bedecked in armour, stepped out in front of me, an axe taller than me clutched in his hand. There was a grin on his face that chilled me to the bone and with his features lit by torchlight, it gave him an almost demonic appearance. The smile only intensified as Dagri skidded to a halt before him and reared up on his hind legs. It was the smile of a man without fear; so confident in his abilities that he felt invincible. This man believed he could not die, and I would have to prove otherwise…

Dagri reared up once more and kicked out at the man, but he merely stumbled back a pace before recovering. With a grin now so wide I was worried he might swallow me whole, the man brushed the dust from his chest where the horse had kicked him, and took a step closer, raising his axe. I could see what was coming and tried to turn, but the press of people all around prevented me. He loomed over us. There was nothing I could do, my sword feeling as useless as a twig in my hand.

The huge man's axe thudded sickeningly into Dagri's neck and with a short, startled, agonised whinny, he collapsed beneath me. I was thrown from his back and landed sprawling in the blood-drenched grass. One of Kichibei's soldiers leapt at me but I thrust my sword upwards, catching the man in his belly before kicking him away from me. I staggered over to the crumpled form of Dagri with tears streaking down my face. His tongue was hanging limply from his mouth and his eyes had rolled up so only the whites showed. I could see at once that he was dead.

I raised my eyes slowly from the body of my friend and companion to look at the man who had taken him from me. He was still leering at me, so confident in himself he had not even bothered to attack while my guard was down. He spoke to me, his voice harsh and guttural, as though unused to our tongue. What he said was barely discernible over the tumult around us, but nevertheless, the words became burned into my memory.

'Aww, did I kill your pretty horsey? What are you going to do about it, boy?'

I gripped my sword handle so tight that it hurt as I strode towards him, my eyes now dry but filled with rage. He seemed pleased with my reaction – to him this was sport…

I was barely half his size, but I was not afraid of him – not even close. He raised his axe as I neared and took a great horizontal swing at me. I ducked swiftly and the blade hissed past my head and crunched into the chest of one of Kichibei's soldiers, his dying scream drowned-out by the huge man's cruel laughter.

He swung at me again and I rolled under the blade towards his legs. Drawing my short sword, I stabbed it into the back of his right thigh, which was not protected by armour. Warm blood spilled over my hand and the man bellowed in agony. He spun and kicked me with his other foot, knocking the breath from my body and sending me barrelling away.

I landed to one side, gasping and choking for air and looked up at him. The smile had left his face and he looked as though he wished to crush my head with his bare hands, which – I reminded myself – he probably could.

I settled into a crouch as he came at me again, his axe raised high. With a snarl he brought it swinging down vertically towards me and I stood and spun to my right in one movement. Before he knew what I was doing I had found a gap in his armour at the waist and stabbed my blade deep into his side, piercing flesh and organs alike. With a scream of rage and pain he brought his fist round and it collided with my head, sending me reeling backwards with shards of light popping before my eyes.

I stumbled and fell – the world spinning around me – all sound seeming muffled and distorted. The man reached down and gripped me by the neck, hauling me high into the air.

'You think that you can beat me!' he shouted into my face, showering me with blood and spittle. 'You are less than an ant to me, less than a grain of dirt, less than a...'

But what else I was less than to him I would not find out, for I had stabbed my sword right through his hand. With an incensed roar he let go and I fell to the floor, rolling between his legs in the same instant. While he was bent over, cradling his ruined hand, I clambered up his back and latched on to his neck. The man bucked like a startled horse and tried to throw me off, but I clung on doggedly. He reached a hand up to grab me but I slashed at it until he withdrew with a yell of pain. I raised my sword in the air and stabbed it deep into the back of his neck – once, twice, three times – the third one cutting straight through his spinal column.

In an instant the man went limp and fell like a tree to the floor, flinging me once more to the dirt. His body twitched gently, then lay still. Dagri's death had been avenged. I could now look for Kamari once more.

With single-minded intensity, I battered my way through the ranks of Kichibei's soldiers, a sword in each hand and my eyes trained on Kamari's back. Wolves were tearing into the enemy all around him, Jaroe and Matai still at his flanks. I noticed a deep, ugly-looking wound down Matai's right side that was oozing blood through his fur. He seemed not to notice it, however, and fought bravely on, bearing his injuries like a true warrior.

'Kamari!' I yelled as loudly as I could. 'Kamari!'

But he could not hear me. I fought closer and closer, yelling his name at the top of my voice and at last I saw him react. He turned and spotted me, slowing his advance to allow me to catch up.

Matai moved aside to make space by my friend and I surveyed his bloody, tattered figure. There was a nasty cut on his left arm and a large bruise around his eye, but other than that he seemed to be alright.

'I was so scared I would be too late, that I... that I would not get a chance to say that I'm...' I began, but Kamari cut me off.

'You don't have to say anything,' he said, punching his sword through a man's chest. 'What was said, was said. It took me a while to realise that our friendship is more important than my word and I should have just been honest with you from the start. Your words hurt me, but I know you would take them back if you could, so I will not let it come between us. We are brothers, and I will never let anything come between us.'

'I am honoured to fight by your side,' I said simply in response.

I clashed my blade with his, then we leapt back into the fight.

We had almost broken through the enemy's ranks to the main gate, where the battering ram was still thudding intermittently into the rapidly degrading door. Away to my left, I watched as Jaroe hurled himself at an enemy, latching his jaws onto the man's face and bearing him to the ground.

'Do we have a plan for when we reach the gate?' I yelled to Kamari over the noise around us.

'Not really, no…' he answered. 'Do you?'

There was only one thing we could do, but it was desperate and dangerous.

Finally, we broke through and stood in an area of open ground before the castle walls. We rushed at the men operating the battering ram, a strange wheeled contraption, and cut them down before they could do any more damage to the gate. The Kurai archers on the wall-top cheered at the sight of us and we waved our weapons in response.

Looking around, I noticed that the ground sloped downwards from the main gate and it had clearly been an effort to propel the ram into the wood each time. I spotted Hanjo fighting nearby and hailed him. He hurried over, panting heavily. Using the incline to our advantage, Kamari, Hanjo and I removed the chocks holding the ram steady and shoved it down the hill into the advancing enemy. It was devastatingly effective, killing many men instantly and wounding many more.

Our army of wolves and men formed-up around the gateway in a vast semi-circle as we figured out what to do. As I had already thought, there was only one thing to do.

'We need to get inside!' I yelled to Kamari, Hanjo, Jaroe and Matai. 'They're too spread out – we'll be slaughtered unless we can force his soldiers to bunch together!'

'What are you saying...?' Kamari asked me.

'We need to open the gates and let them follow us in,' I replied.

CHAPTER SEVENTEEN

For a moment Kamari looked at me aghast, then his face cleared.

'You're right,' he said. 'We have to get the gates open.'

With Hanjo and I guarding him, Kamari turned and yelled up at the archers on the wall-top, signalling our intentions to them. From what I could see of their faces, they did not seem too impressed by our plan. An argument broke out between several of the archers, then all at once they turned as though they had been hailed. Their heads disappeared from view and I turned back to the fight raging around me.

'They had better hurry,' I said through gritted teeth, watching as an arrow took a wolf through the chest, his howl cut suddenly short. Beside me, Jaroe panted wearily, blood dripping from his jaws. He dodged a thrust from a spear and leapt at the carrier.

Looking out over the battle, I could see that both sides were now severely depleted. Countless torches – that had so recently been carried by men – now lay on the grass, extinguishing themselves in pools of blood and rainwater. Weapons and bodies were scattered everywhere – trampled and muddy – the corpses causing more deaths amongst our enemy as men tripped and were trampled or fell upon dropped blades. I looked to the horizon and saw that it would soon be dawn, when the true horror and barbarity of this battle would be revealed to us.

I was snapped-out of my musings by the dull grating of the crossbar being lifted from the gate behind me and slowly – oh, so slowly – the doors were tugged open, splinters of wood falling from the hole that had been punched at their centre.

'Everyone inside!' I yelled to our army in both the common and the wolf tongue.

Not needing a second bidding, they began to move – backing as fast as possible towards the gateway with Kichibei's men close behind them. I led the way through the gate and was greeted by the remnants of the Kurai, who had split their forces between the wall-tops and the gate. Shjin was among them.

I hurried towards him and he clasped my hand as I reached him, gripping it tightly and smiling at me in a fatherly way.

'I have to say, many here did not think you would return in time,' he said.

'Well, I'm here now,' I replied, trying to mirror his smile. 'We need to get ourselves formed-up if we want to survive this.'

Shjin nodded and signalled to his archers.

'Form two ranks – first rank fires while the second rank reloads. Wait for my signal once Kichibei's men bunch-up in the gateway.'

I was just about to move off and rejoin Kamari when I heard a familiar voice behind me.

'You have done us all proud,' the voice said. I spun around to see Lord Orran approaching me. 'Your timing was a little off, but you are here nevertheless.'

I was not sure, but I think he meant the last part humorously; it was difficult to determine any emotions beneath the worn and tired exterior of a man whose end might soon be upon him. He seemed to age dramatically every time I saw him, as though he was withering away before my eyes. Here stood a man who was facing the end of his bloodline – the end of his reign as lord of this domain. It was a heavy burden for any man to bear and grief and worry appeared to have all but finished him. I bowed low before him, but did not know what to say.

'No,' he said suddenly. 'Please do not bow before me, stand.' I stood and raised my face to look at him. 'You do not bow to me – not now, not ever.' He looked down at me kindly and gripped my shoulder with one hand. 'Now go, your army needs you,' he added, taking a step back behind the ranks of archers. I nodded to him and hurried to stand by Kamari.

Kichibei's men had taken the bait and were even now beginning to mass in the gateway, driven recklessly onward by their lord's lust for power and revenge. Shjin's archers began to fire volley after volley over the heads of our army into the enemy, but still they came.

To my left I watched Hanjo leap into the path of an enemy soldier who was lunging at a downed wolf. He barely deflected the blade in time, its tip instead finding Hanjo's upper arm and tearing it open. With a yell, Hanjo buried his sword in the man's stomach and hurled him backwards. A short distance away I spotted Matai staring at him. He stood still over the body of his latest victim, breathing heavily, looking at Hanjo as though seeing him for the first time.

Kamari handed me a bow and quiver and standing together at the rear of our army, we began to loose arrows quickly and accurately into the oncoming enemy. But it was becoming dangerous to fire arrows from our current position; I was worried I would hit our own men, so Kamari and I retreated further up the slope to gain higher ground. From this elevated position, I could see through the wide-open gates, over the heads of the advancing soldiers and across the scene of devastation behind them.

And there he was.

It could be no other.

Kichibei sat astride his war horse flanked by a vanguard of six generals, urging his army to victory with frenzied waves and encouraging shouts. His armour was stunningly elaborate, beautiful in its craft but terrifying in appearance, lit as it was by torchlight. His helmet was shaped in the likeness of a dragon and the light of the flames held by his generals made it appear to be alive. Such fine armour for one who would not be engaging in battle, I thought scornfully.

I was about to loose another arrow when something caught my eye amongst the ranks of Kichibei's soldiers and I moved to take a closer look. Heads were turning as something grey streaked above them, bounding over their heads using shoulders and skulls as stepping stones.

It cannot be, I thought in astonishment.

But it was…

Meera leapt down and wove her way between the legs of our troops until she stood on the other side and caught sight of me. She ran towards me and, as though in a dream, I knelt down to embrace her – delighted, amazed and terrified all at once.

'What… what are you doing here? You could have been killed!' I said falteringly, looking into her eyes. 'You know how important you are, you are not supposed to risk yourself,' I added, hearing myself say the words, but unable to stem the flow of joy that filled me at the sight of her. 'Why did you come here? How did you escape your guards?'

She looked at me and sighed, as though I might not understand what she was about to say.

'It just felt right,' she replied. 'I knew that I was meant to be here, I always knew that my path would lead me here… because this is where you are.'

'But…' I began.

'Our paths run side by side, Takashi,' she said, before I could finish. 'My place is by your side – that is where our paths are leading us and nothing will stand in the way of that, my "destiny" to be the Soul

Channel included. I never asked for this role and never wanted it. I now see that everything has led up to this moment, from the time I died saving you to now – it was all part of it. Everything has led to this point, but I have realised that destiny is not set in stone. There is always a choice and for however long it may last – however fleeting it may be – I have chosen to forget everything, to forget it all and be with you, my love.'

Tears were falling down my cheeks, tears of happiness and relief and love; amidst the chaos around us I wept.

'I realised all this whilst standing with my guards, watching from the forest,' she continued. 'I felt deep inside that where I stood was not where I was meant to be. I had to regain my true path. I considered fighting the guards, but could see how badly they wanted to join the battle. It did not take much convincing to make them realise it was where all three of us were meant to be. Their destinies were to fight with their brothers and mine is to be by your side, now and forever.'

'There is nowhere else I would rather be,' I said, wiping my eyes. 'But to be honest, I didn't think I would ever see you again… I never thought you would try to come here and after… I… I thought Jaroe would keep you from me…'

'I believe that is what he intends to do,' Meera replied, smiling and showing rows of gleaming fangs. 'But I don't answer to Jaroe – I answer only to myself.'

As though he had heard us over the sounds of battle, Jaroe appeared at our side – feelings of shock and fear radiating from him.

'Meera!' he said in astonishment. 'What are you doing here? Do you have any idea how much danger you are in?'

'Yes,' she replied quietly, looking up at me. Jaroe flicked his gaze between the two of us, then turned to me, anger plain in his voice.

'This is your fault,' he said, a snarl curling his lips. 'If she dies it will be upon your head!'

'No, it was not my choice for her to come here. Do you think I would willingly put her in danger?' I retorted. 'She made a choice. The fault here is your belief that any will other than her own brought her here. It is not for you – or anyone else – to impose their will upon her, and you or your Council cannot pretend to know what is best for her. None of you has any right to try and control her.'

Jaroe looked as though he wanted to say more, but instead he merely hung his head and sighed.

'There is some truth in what you say,' he said, his voice mournful, as though Meera had already died. 'The life of the Soul Channel is a difficult one… Just look after her and please… make sure no harm comes to her.'

He was turning away from us when a great howl was heard coming from the gateway; many wolf voices united as one in their shock and grief. It was a heart-wrenching sound, and as the howls died away an almost complete silence blanketed the area. It lasted only a moment before furious snarls snatched away the quiet.

'Something's happened,' Jaroe said worriedly, darting back down to the gate with Meera and I following swiftly after.

A body lay in the dirt, surrounded by a wall of wolves and men, protecting the fallen. A short sword protruded from its chest and blood pooled around it, soaking the soft grey fur that had so recently risen and fallen with the rhythm of life. Hanjo knelt by the side of the wolf, a hand resting on its shoulder.

Jaroe had stopped still, his eyes wide and terrified. He threw back his head and bayed the pain of his loss and woe to the sky. He stepped forward brokenly and laid a paw on the wolf's side, nudging his neck with his muzzle as if trying to wake him. But Matai would never rise again.

'I should have been with you, brother,' he whispered into his dead friend's ear. 'I should have been at your side.'

He howled once more, then stood and hurled himself through the protective wall around Matai, wild in his attempts to wreak retribution upon his enemy. I walked over and stood beside Hanjo. His eyes were red and swollen and when he looked up at me, I saw confusion in them.

'He... the wolf, he... he saved me...' Hanjo whispered. 'One of Kichibei's men got behind me and I... I hadn't noticed him. The first I knew of it was when I heard a grunt behind me. The wolf had jumped into the path of his blade. Even with the sword sticking out of him, he still managed to turn and take down the man, I… I've never seen endurance quite like it. Then he stumbled back here and fell… he was dead within seconds of hitting the floor…'

Hanjo's voice cracked and he looked away from me.

I looked down at Matai's body and felt a strange mix of emotions at the sight. Here lay the creature responsible for many of the problems I had faced over the past few days. He was the reason the Council had not leapt to help Lord Orran from the start. He was the one who had caused the division in the Council and stubbornly stated that Lord Orran would not receive aid until their own problem was solved. If he had just agreed to help me from the start, then… then maybe things would have been different, maybe…

But I understood and accepted the reasons for everything he had done. It is not always easy to see the consequences of the decisions we make. Matai did what he believed was best for his brothers and sisters – his family – and I knew first-hand just how hard it was to choose between loyalties and loved ones.

I could not feel angry with him for how things had turned out. In the end, he had done the right thing – or at least what *I* believed to be the right thing – for clearly it had not been right for him, for here he now lay, never to run with his family again. In the end, he had managed to show his loyalties to both his duty and his family; he had fought for both, and he had died for both.

I knelt down and laid a hand on Matai's neck.

'Thank you,' I whispered.

I stood then and, with Meera at my side, joined my comrades holding-off the enemy in the gateway.

We had managed to push them back past the halfway point of the gateway tunnel, but for every man we killed and every finger-length of ground we gained, more of Kichibei's soldiers would pop up to push back against us. I slashed at a face that suddenly leered in front of me, ducking low to sweep my blade at ankle-height, felling several men who would either bleed to death or have the life trampled from them. Picking up a spear dropped by one of Kichibei's men, I hurled it into the enemy – the shaft pinning two men together through their chests. To my right, Meera latched her jaws into a man's wrist and dragged him screaming to the ground, where she pounced at his face. When she re-emerged, her muzzle was crimson.

'They taste foul,' she said, bringing a smile to my lips. Jaroe had told me to protect her, but I think it was Kichibei's men who needed protecting from her.

'Kamari!' I yelled across at my friend, who was fighting side by side with Shjin. The two of them extricated themselves from the battle and ran over.

'We need to press our advantage,' I yelled over the hubbub. 'We have to organise the troops on the wall-tops.' Shjin looked as though he was thinking quickly. He motioned to several archers.

'Come with me.'

Together we hurried up the wall steps and looked down upon Kichibei's forces massing around the gate. I looked up and down the walls and realised that most of the men who had been stationed here had gone down to join the fight below. Several heavy iron pots of oil were bubbling gently over small fires lined along the walls and it was obvious what we had to do.

'We need to position these pots over the gateway,' Shjin said, indicating that we should do so with the help of the archers. Nodding in agreement, we moved off down the walls.

It was difficult and dangerous moving the pots of oil. The handles were blazingly hot and we had to use leather pads to grip them, which quickly became slippery with sweat. On numerous occasions I stumbled with the weight of the thing, just managing to keep a grip on the slick leather. My heart was pounding excruciatingly fast after so many near fatal slips.

Eventually we had the pots lined up above Kichibei's soldiers, who were still trying to force their way inside the castle. The heat from the pots singed my face and I almost felt sorry for the men below. Almost.

'Alright, we need to tip these simultaneously over the battlements,' Shjin said, looking at each of us in turn. 'Two men per pot, we tip them on my command. Now lift them into position.'

Kamari and I reached down to grasp a handle each and carefully hauled it up and rested it against the stone.

'Everybody ready?' Shjin asked, preparing to give the command. I was about to reply when I felt a sudden pounding in my head, and my world went dark.

'I... I can't see,' I mumbled, glancing blindly around.

'Now! Tip them!' I heard Shjin shout.

'You don't need to see!' I heard Kamari say as if from nowhere. 'Just tip!'

I did as he told me and tipped the heavy pot over the battlement, releasing my hold and allowing the pot to fall to earth as the hot liquid spilled out. Agonised, tortured screams tore upwards from below as the boiling liquid blistered the flesh of Kichibei's troops. But I did not hear them for long. I felt blood rushing painfully around my head as I slid down the stone wall behind me and crumpled in a heap on the battlements.

CHAPTER EIGHTEEN

'Takashi! Takashi! Are you alright?' Kamari was slapping me gently in the face, trying to wake me.

'Wha… what happened?' I asked groggily.

'You… you must have blacked-out for a minute there… You just collapsed after tipping the oil,' he answered, concern evident in his voice. 'You need to rest – you can't go on like this. You haven't slept for days, you've barely eaten – your body cannot take this much longer!'

'I can't rest yet!' I said, struggling awkwardly to my feet. 'I need to… I need to…'

I looked over the battlements and saw the horrific destruction the hot oil had inflicted on our enemy. The grass was ablaze in many places, the oil having ignited upon contact with the enemy's torches. Soldiers writhed on the ground like snakes in their torment, the boiling oil unleashing many slow, painful deaths among our foe. Here and there, flames licked at corpses and I noticed men rolling around to put out fires on their clothing.

'I need to...' I said again, not sure what I was going to say and still feeling decidedly woozy. 'Where is Meera?' I asked at last, looking around me.

'She is still down at the gate,' Kamari replied, following me as I tottered down the wall steps.

'Meera!' I yelled, setting my head thudding once again. She detached herself from the throng in the gateway and ran towards us.

'I think you've done it!' she said excitedly, 'I think you've turned the battle in our favour, I... what has happened?' she asked, suddenly anxious as she looked at me.

'I... I blacked-out,' I replied, deciding on the truth. 'Kamari thinks I should rest, but he doesn't understand...'

Meera looked up at me and I noticed a strange light in her eyes.

'He is just concerned for your wellbeing,' she said, her voice sounding odd to me. 'But *I* understand why you won't rest yet – why you can't rest yet. Maybe sometime soon your friend will understand too.'

Wordlessly, Kamari, Meera and I re-joined the battle.

Meera was right – the battle had indeed turned in our favour. The boiling oil had done its job and Kichibei's soldiers were scattered and demoralised. Only Kichibei's frenzied yells and furious threats bullied them into continuing the fight. But they knew it was over, and so did we.

Slowly we began to push them back, out into the open plain where they had nowhere to hide, and one by one we began to cut them down with blades and arrows. I stabbed and sliced at men around me who put up little resistance to their fates. They were on the verge of fleeing and soon even the fear of their lord would not prevent them from doing so.

Kichibei seemed to have realised this. I saw him in the distance, his face livid with rage beneath his dragon helmet. With a savage yell he broke free of his generals and began to charge alone towards the gate, his sword raised.

Next to me, Meera tensed as she saw Kichibei approach and, with a growl rumbling deep in her throat, she sprinted after him.

'No, Meera, wait!' I yelled after her, but she ignored me.

Kichibei's generals had given chase and had almost caught him – they would kill her unless I stopped them. I yelled at Kamari, Hanjo, Tamoe and Shjin – who were fighting nearby – and they joined me as I rushed to cut off the six generals on horseback.

With Meera still chasing Kichibei, we just managed to get between her and the generals before they were upon us. The man in the lead tried to ride me down, driving his horse recklessly towards me. With less than a second to think, I rolled to one side and held my blade high, feeling it sever the straps of the man's saddle. I turned quickly to watch him slide from his horse and crunch to the ground where his horse's hooves connected with his neck, breaking it instantly. The other five generals reined their horses to a halt before us and dismounted.

Once on the ground, the five men removed their helmets and bowed to us. For a second, I thought they were going to surrender, but then they raised their weapons and rushed us – yelling war cries.

I knew I should stay with Kamari and the others – for I did not want to leave them outnumbered – but I had to check that Meera was alright. Glancing behind me, I saw that she had engaged Kichibei in combat. She leapt around, dodging the slashes from his blade and the hooves of his startled horse as it reared above her. I began to move towards her when I heard a shout of pain.

Spinning around, I was just in time to see Tamoe fall to the dirt, a great patch of crimson spreading across his cream kimono. The general who had killed him withdrew his dripping blade and inclined his head mockingly to Shjin. I could not desert them now.

Enraged by the death of our comrade, the four of us hacked brutally at the five generals, who were driven back by our ferocity. Using his sword handle as a weapon, Shjin punched one of the men repeatedly in the face until his nose broke beneath his fist. As he staggered backwards, spitting blood, Shjin slid his sword beneath the man's armour and drove the blade deep into his gut. Momentarily distracted, I did not manage to deflect a blow that ripped open my right arm, leaving my haori hanging off me in bloody tatters.

With Kamari by my side, we battered my attacker backwards until he tripped and fell to the ground, weakly parrying the blows that hammered down upon him. With a deft flick, Kamari sent his blade spinning off into the grass some distance away and as one, we drove our blades into him. The dying man's legs kicked briefly so we stabbed down once more. Only three of the generals remained.

'The fight is a fair one now,' I said, panting like a winded dog. 'I have to go and help Meera.' Kamari nodded in understanding.

'Go,' he said, turning back to the fight. I faltered for just a second, then ran after Meera.

Meera was in trouble. Kichibei was leaning out of his saddle and slashing powerfully at her, his aged appearance hiding a surprising well of strength. He had already inflicted several wounds upon her but still she fought on, snapping at his hand whenever she could dodge the blade. I was pleased to realise she had managed to wound him too, for his hand was now bleeding profusely. I hurtled towards her, nothing else in my head other than the desire to stand by her side.

Her attention was so focussed on Kichibei and his sword that she did not see the horse's hoof hurtling towards her until it was too late. It connected with her chest and threw her to the floor where she lay, gasping in pain and sucking in air through her damaged windpipe.

I heard Kichibei laugh victoriously and watched as he raised his sword to finish his downed foe. I stopped breathing. Time seemed to grind to a halt as a sudden, terrible thought struck me. Pieces of the puzzle began to drop into place as I looked at this scene. Was this what it had meant all along? Was this what the feeling of inevitability had been leading to? Had this always been the conclusion – the end of my path? The figure of the wolf I had seen so many times at night, I had thought I recognised it… Was it… was it Meera? Had it been a warning? Was she about to die? Was I never meant to be with her after all?

It could not be. How could this be the end to which my path – *our paths* – had brought us? After all we had fought through, this could not be how it all ended. It could not be… I would not let it end this way.

My strength was almost spent but I forced my body onwards, desperate to prevent what I now took to be inevitable. I could see his blade scything towards her, hungry to bite flesh and split bone, and knew she was too injured to dodge it this time. There was only one choice left open to me – one decision left to make – and I made it gladly, automatically, without a second thought.

I threw myself before the gaze of his ravenous blade and it accepted its new target readily, biting deep into the warm flesh of my stomach, tasting my blood and intestines. I fell against Meera who was breathing shallowly. She struggled to stand, but collapsed back to the earth and lay still. Kichibei sneered down at me from his horse.

'Honourable,' he said mockingly, staring at me down his hooked nose. 'But foolish.'

He raised his sword for the final blow, but as he brought it swinging towards me, I reached out suddenly and gripped his wrist, tugging him savagely from his horse. He landed awkwardly in the grass by my side, his foot caught in one of the stirrups.

I was on top of him before he could react. I gripped him by the front of his armour and head-butted him over and over until my forehead and hair were matted with his blood. Somehow, he managed to bring his knee up and catch me directly in my stomach wound and I rolled off him, screaming in pain as I felt it tear wider. Kichibei kicked his foot free of the stirrup and with a hand clamped to his ruined, bloody face, cast around for his weapon.

His eyes gleamed as they fell upon his sword, sticking out of the grass nearby. He stumbled towards it and pulled it free of the earth, walking slowly back towards my prone form.

'I'm going to enjoy killing you,' Kichibei said thickly through a mouthful of blood. He looked over at Meera still lying winded in the grass and spat upon the floor. 'And your little friend there. I think

I'll cut her legs and tail off before I finish her,' he ended, his face creasing in a bloodstained smile.

I gripped the blade lying concealed at my side and looked up at Shigako Kichibei. All of a sudden, I began to laugh as I looked into the face of my enemy.

'Have I said something that amuses you, boy?' he asked furiously.

I did not say anything in response, I simply continued to laugh. Soon, Kichibei began to laugh too; a mirthless, terrible sound that drowned out my laughter as he took a step closer and raised his sword above his head.

'Let's see if you're still laughing a few seconds from now,' he hissed.

He was about to bring the blade down upon my neck when I made my move. Mustering the last of my strength, I sat bolt upright and forced my sword through his chest. His mouth agape, Kichibei teetered on the spot as I withdrew the blade with a sickening sound and a fountain of blood.

For a few seconds I thought he was sure to fall, then he seemed to regain his balance, the ghost of a sneer on his lips, blood drooling down his chin. Raising his sword once more, Kichibei brought the blade down, even as the breath was dying in his throat, the sneer fading, the light leaving his eyes.

I could see the point of his sword descending ever closer to my neck, but try as I might, I could not force my limbs to move. I could not roll to one side or deflect the blow – I could not seem to do anything at all to stop it. All the rushing around of the past few weeks, all the sleepless nights, all the worry and grief and pain since I had set out from Harakima what seemed like years ago, had finally taken their toll on me. But it was something more than simple tiredness. My body was spent and that feeling of inevitability pervaded every shred of my being.

I had been wrong before. So very, very wrong. It had not been that moment that was inevitable, but this one. This was meant to be; everything, *everything* I had done – every decision I had made under the influence of this feeling – had led up to this point, and I knew what I had to do. I would give myself up to that side of me; the side I had only ever tapped into a few times before, the side that frightened and confused me, but also intrigued and excited me. My wolf side. My true side. This was where my path had been leading all along. This was where my path ended, and a new one began…

The blade was inches from my neck when a blur of grey shot past me and I heard Kichibei grunt in pain. I looked on as Meera bore the struggling Kichibei to the ground and with one short, sharp bite, tore out his throat.

It was done.

It was finally over. But it was too late for me.

I felt my eyes beginning to cloud over and everything around me became dim and indistinct. The last thing I saw was Meera hurrying back towards me where she lay down at my side and placed her forepaws on my chest.

'Stand up.'

I opened my eyes and looked around. At first, I could see nothing clearly, for everything still seemed to blur and shimmer before me. I sat up slowly and spotted the speaker. The black wolf I had seen so many times before stared intently at me from the nearby tree line. I stood up and walked shakily towards it, the light of recognition slowly dawning upon me. Meera padded along at my side, her eyes fixed upon the dark wolf ahead of us.

I knew who this was before I even reached him. I think I had always known, really, deep down. I had sensed something about him the first time I had seen him, sitting between the trees on the opposite bank to my camp. When Jaroe and Matai described the origins of the Soul Channel it had sounded familiar, but for some reason I had forgotten my history. But seeing him now, it all came flooding back. I knew my ancestor when I saw him.

'Timaeo,' I whispered, overawed. The original Soul Channel nodded in agreement.

'Come,' he said, his voice quiet and reassuring. 'It is time.'

I looked out across the plains to where Kamari was still mopping-up the last of Kichibei's soldiers, then looked down at Meera sitting next to me. I knelt before her and hugged her tight before pressing my forehead against hers. Then I stood and silently followed Timaeo off into the darkness between the trees.

The time had come for me to choose, would I sleep… or would I run?

CHAPTER NINETEEN

I cannot let the story end here, for there is more to tell of the events that followed the passing of my friend... my brother, Takashi Asano. We found his body lying out in the mud of the battlefield next to the corpse of the slain Lord Kichibei. Wolf prints led away from my friend's body into the tree line, but when we went to search the forest, there was no sign of any wolves and Meera was nowhere to be found.

For several days I was unable to talk and barely able to move as grief consumed me. I simply lay on my mat in a guest house in Harakima and wept for my friend. It took me all that time to realise what a fool I was to grieve for him. Afterwards my behaviour made me feel as though I did not know him at all. It took me a long time to realise that Takashi would not wish me to grieve for him, for he was finally where he wanted to be. I had known all along that his path would lead him wherever Meera's led her, for they walked a path that was one and the same. I knew he would always follow her, even into death; for death for him was the path to a new beginning, and that seemed the only way they could truly be together.

From that point on, I no longer felt sadness at the death of my friend. I felt happy for him. Just as I had seemed destined to end up with Ellia, I knew that Takashi and Meera were meant for each other – whatever the sacrifice, in whatever form – they were always meant to be together, and that was a heartening thought.

A funeral was planned for my friend and all those who had died in the battle against Lord Kichibei. But before it could go ahead, I had one very important thing to do. And so it was that one fine morning I packed up a cloth sack full of food and water and climbed into the saddle of a fine, strong horse. It was young and had not yet been named and Lord Orran – who by now looked a lot healthier and much less care-worn – allowed me to name it. I chose to call the horse Dagri, in honour of the companion who had accompanied us throughout our long and arduous adventures, and who had sadly died on the field of battle. Astride my new friend, I set out from the castle town towards the village I had grown up in, to deliver news I had hoped never to have to utter.

The ride was uneventful apart from a strange incident that occurred one night after I had set up camp by the banks of a stream. I had eaten a meal of rice and fish and drunk a cupful of fresh water before settling down to rest with the newly-named Dagri tethered to a tree nearby. I had been sleeping peacefully when, for no apparent reason, I awoke all of a sudden.

At first, I had been unable to discern what had woken me. There was not a sound to be heard anywhere and normally I slept as deeply as an animal in hibernation. It was as I was about to lie down and fall asleep once more that I saw them, or at least thought I saw them. I cannot be sure; I think perhaps my eyes were playing tricks on me. But what I thought I saw were the shapes of two wolves sitting side by side just beyond the tree line. Shadows enveloped them, so it was difficult to tell if they were real or constructs of my imagination, but I felt at once something familiar about them. I knew who I so badly wanted these wolves to be, but when – in the blink of an eye – they disappeared, I found it hard to convince myself I had really seen anything. This may sound as though I am trying to convince you – or perhaps myself – but I am simply relating what occurred as honestly as I can.

When I finally arrived in Aigano, the silence was the first thing that struck me. I was so used to it being a bustling hive of activity that seeing it deserted made it take on an entirely different aura. I walked through the village like one in a dream, recalling times past when I had played and sparred with Takashi. I remembered his fumbling attempts at sword fighting and how easily I had been able to disarm him. It became so embarrassing that I eventually took it upon myself to teach him in the use of the sword, for I trained far longer and harder than he ever did. It brought a smile to my face to think how that clumsy little boy had gone on to lead an army of wolves and men into battle.

As I walked past the empty animal pens, I remembered the time an ox escaped from its pen and caused havoc in the village, knocking over baskets of rice and upsetting buckets of water. The beast appeared demented and no one had been able to calm it enough to capture it. Takashi and I had taken it upon ourselves to catch the poor animal, as it was only going to hurt itself if allowed to continue. Using one of the fishing nets from the river, we weighted it down by tying heavy stones to it and clambered onto the roofs of two houses that stood opposite each other.

Signalling our plan to the villagers, we got them to drive the ox slowly but surely towards the gap between the houses we sat upon. After waiting patiently for over an hour, the ox at last passed beneath us and we pushed the rocks off the roof, which dragged the heavy net with them and trapped the beast beneath it.

We had been heroes that day, Takashi and I, and our capture had been the talk of the village for days after. I shook my head and smiled at all the happy memories that surrounded this place, but I could not forget the many sad memories it held also. I still find it amazing how a single place can inspire such different and wildly varying emotions in a person.

I walked into Takashi's house at last, not knowing what I would find within. Takashi's mother sat on a cushion in the middle of the main room, staring expectantly at the door as I entered. By her side sat a man I did not recognise. His hair and beard were long and white and his faded kimono was wrapped tightly around him to keep out the chill.

'We have been waiting for you,' the man said, before I had a chance to ask his name. 'You come bearing news.'

'Yes, I do, but...' I turned to Takashi's mother and sighed; my eyes downcast – the news I had to relate eating me up inside. 'I'm so, so very sorry to have to tell you this, but... Takashi has... passed on...'

Takashi's mother did not react as I expected. She did not cry, she did not even flinch at the news; she merely smiled wanly in acceptance, as though she had known this all along. She had a faraway look in her eyes when next she spoke, as though she could see through the walls and out into the sky above.

'Passed on... that is a nice way to put it,' she said almost dreamily. 'He has moved on from one life to another, a new beginning for him and his love. But I do not think we have seen the last of him and we will always carry him here with us,' she said, laying a hand on her breast.

'A funeral has been planned for him and the others that died during battle - I think... I think he would like it if you were there,' I said.

'Yes...' she said in answer. 'Yes, I think he would.'

'Good, then would you like to accompany me back to the castle? Of course, you may come too, sir,'

I said, switching my gaze to the man seated cross-legged at her side.

'No, thank you, I have other places to be,' the man said, as he stood and picked up a cloth bag that lay nearby. I moved to help Takashi's mother stand up, but before I got there she had already got steadily to her feet.

'As you can see, I am feeling much better,' she said with a smile.

I took her arm in mine and walked her out of the house towards Dagri, who I had tied-up by the front steps. The old man followed us out and began to walk northwards along the bank towards the bridge. Takashi's mother hailed him as he walked.

'Will we see each other again?' she asked.

'Oh… I expect we shall,' he replied.

I helped Takashi's mother into the saddle, then climbed up myself and set off at a steady pace back towards Harakima.

Two days later the funeral was held. The weather had stayed fine and the sun shone down brightly upon the rows of bodies that lay wrapped on individual funeral pyres. The bodies of the wolves who had died during battle had also been wrapped – with the aid of several villagers from Harakima – and subsequently dragged-off for a private burial by the Council. I wondered if I would ever understand their mysterious ways. The one person I could have asked about it was now gone, but some things are not for me to know. Some mysteries must simply remain that... a mystery.

There had still been no sight or sound of Meera, and as I said, I had no way to ask them about it. I could not ask whether they were going to send scouts after her... after Takashi too. So instead I just had to hope that wherever they were now, they were together, and I prayed to the spirits that Jaroe and the Council would leave them be and not hunt them down to retrieve their Soul Channel.

Other than the wolves, everyone that survived the battle attended the funeral – from the dock workers and Hanjo's men, to the remainder of the Kurai, who were by now bordering on extinction. Gifts and tokens were laid upon many of the bodies and there were plentiful tears shed that day. I stood side by side with Ellia and Takashi's mother, looking down at my brother's body. Prayers were said by friends and family, thanking the fallen for giving their lives for the safety of the domain and wishing them a peaceful passage from this life to the next.

Lord Orran himself came down to the funeral – dressed in his finest armour – to offer his thanks to the soldiers who had fought and died for him. He looked extremely humble as he stood before the ranks of funeral pyres and when he spoke, the humility he felt was clear as day in his voice.

'I was honoured to stand in the presence of each and every one of these heroic warriors, who are sadly no longer with us,' he said quietly, his voice somehow still managing to carry across the gathering. 'An old fool like me does not deserve such unwavering bravery and loyalty. In life they bowed before me, and now, I do so before them.'

Drawing gasps from several people, Lord Orran dropped to his knees and bowed low before the deceased.

Slowly, every man, woman and child gathered there that morning followed suit, bowing to the floor to honour the fallen. There was not a sound anywhere, only the wind blowing through the grass as each person knelt quietly, wrapped-up in their own thoughts and memories.

From behind us, away in the distance, a great howl went up, carrying towards us on the wind. We all stood and turned to look out over the western wall towards a great grey mass that stood with their noses pointed to the clear blue sky.

The wolves had come to pay their respects.

Right then I wished more than ever that I could understand the wolf tongue, for the song they howled was the most beautiful thing I had ever heard. It was haunting and mournful, but at the same time it was filled with hope and joy – a celebration of the lives of those brave souls now gone. It brought a tear to my eye and that song has stuck with me ever since. I still hum it now and then in the dead of night, when my thoughts turn to the adventures Takashi and I shared over those chaotic few months.

All at once the song ceased and the wolves retreated back into the trees. As sad as it may sound,

I hoped against hope I would never see them again, for if I ever did, it would most likely mean we had reached a new period of war, and I pray every night that I will never be involved in another battle.

We all turned back as the funeral ceremony drew near its end. The likenesses of wolves made of folded paper were placed upon the bodies, the purpose of which was to speed the passing of the few brave souls deemed worthy enough to be reborn in the skin of a wolf.

The pyres were lit and as the flames licked around the bodies, more tears were shed into the grass beneath our feet. Ellia moved closer to me and I hugged her to my side, feeling her body quivering with emotion. As I looked at the tongues of red-orange flame that slowly devoured Takashi's body, I was almost certain I discerned a shape there. I have never said this to anyone before – so I wish you to keep this between us – but deep within the flames I would swear I saw a wolf's head staring out at me, its features proud and noble and a smile obvious on its lips. I looked down at Ellia to see if she had noticed it, but her eyes were closed as tears trickled out from beneath the lids.

I looked instead at Takashi's mother and saw a knowing smile on her lips as tears fell slowly down her face. To this day I do not know if she saw what I saw, but I certainly do not think that vision was intended just for me.

In the days following the funeral some good news reached my ears – both Takai and Shjin received official pardons from Lord Orran! For his help in retrieving the Soul Channel, Takai has had his terrible mistake forgiven and both he and his family have been invited to return to Harakima – I believe he is now searching for them to deliver the glad tidings. As for Shjin, for his bravery and valour in fighting off Kichibei's forces he too has been given a full pardon and earned back the respect he lost. Like Takai, he has been invited to make Harakima his home once more but has decided – for now at least – to return to Harani with his family.

Several months later my wife Ellia went into labour with the first of our offspring. The birth was extremely hard on her and many believed she would not survive the night. Wracked with worry, I paced up and down outside the birthing room, each fresh scream of pain feeling like a knife being twisted deeper and deeper in my heart. I knew deep down that if she did not survive the birth then it would not be long before I followed her into death. I could not live without her, it was as simple as that, and the thought that I could lose both her and my child tore me up inside.

At last I heard the first screams of a healthy baby and my heart leapt within me. I waited patiently to be permitted to enter the room, but after half an hour had passed and I had not been called, I began to get anxious again. Had something gone wrong?

Were they even now trying to bring her back from the brink of death?

I had been nibbling a fingernail and it was only when I tasted iron that I realised my finger was bleeding. Several times I almost burst into the room to see what was going on, but each time I stopped myself, for my wife had asked me specifically not to enter, as she did not wish me to see her in this state.

Then I heard a sound I had not expected to hear. A second baby's voice joined the first and my stomach turned over in shock and joy as I realised the truth.

'You may come in now,' a female voice said at last.

I barrelled into the room to see my wife sitting up on her blanket-strewn mat, cradling a baby in each arm. She was crying, but it was not from the pain of the labour she had just been through – she was crying with happiness.

'Kamari,' she said through her sobs. 'We have twins, a boy and a girl.'

I stumbled over to her and sat down on the mat, overcome with emotion.

'They're beautiful,' I whispered, bending to kiss Ellia's forehead. As I withdrew, I reached out and gently stroked each of my children's heads in turn, feeling their skin warm and soft against my palm.

'I love you,' I said to Ellia, staring gratefully into her eyes.

'Well, I hope so,' she said with a weak smile. 'Because we're going to have our hands full.'

The celebration of the birth of my two perfect children went on for an entire day and a more splendid occasion I had never known (apart from my wedding of course – but don't tell Ellia I put the birthday celebration first). People from villages all around came to congratulate us and offer gifts. However, the question on everybody's lips was – what were we going to call the children? But Ellia and I had already agreed that we would save the naming for a special time and place.

By this point most of the Aigano villagers had already moved back home, now the threat of Kichibei was gone. Ellia and I had only stayed in Harakima because she had been heavily pregnant and travel would have been ill-advised. Takashi's mother had taken Mia back with her to Aigano and her daughter had been very sad to leave because she did not want to miss the birth of the babies. But I promised her she could help take care of them once we returned to Aigano.

However, many of the villagers had visited for the birthday party so there was no end of volunteers to help with our trip home. A horse-drawn cart was given to us by Lord Orran so Ellia and the children could ride in comfort. We packed them in with blankets until they could barely move, loaded up with supplies, said our goodbyes, and left the castle town at last.

Two days later, we arrived back in Aigano. We had taken the journey slow and enjoyed our time together on the road, but now we were just glad to be home. We unpacked our things and made the babies comfortable, then together Ellia and I waited for night to fall. We talked about many things; we laughed, joked and cried together as the hours drifted away, seated on the steps outside our house and listening to the whispering of the trees.

In the hour before the spirits awoke, we roused the babes and quietly carried them out to the bridge that crossed the river. Ellia held our son and I held our daughter. We had sought out the blessings of both Takashi's mother and Lord Orran before planning this naming ceremony and now – even though I could not explain it – the time felt right.

'Welcome to your new home, Meera,' I said to the baby in my arms.

'And welcome to your new home, Takashi,' Ellia said to the child in hers. 'We want to tell you the story of your name-sakes. It is a tale of forbidden love between two people who should never ordinarily have met. It is a tale of high adventure; of hardship, grief and pain, but more than anything else, it is a tale that assures us that if you believe in something strongly enough, then not even death can stand in your way. It is a tale of two great people, our friends, Takashi Asano and Meera Orran.'

EPILOGUE

Soft grass beneath our pads. The sun on our backs. The warm wind ruffling our fur. Meera and I ran side by side, together at last. After everything we had been through, we were finally united, running next to each other as though an army were chasing us; not caring in which direction we were running, but simply running for the sake of it, allowing our legs to take us wherever they would – just as I had promised all that time ago.

That life now seemed an eternity ago, but one thing I was sure of was I would never forget the love and loyalty of the friends and family I had known throughout that life. I would check in on my family and Kamari from time to time, but for the moment my world consisted only of Meera and the ground beneath my feet. I felt at last that I had found my place in life. I no longer felt like I was drifting and I knew it was because of the strong spirit that ran beside me.

We both knew that we could not keep running forever, we knew that someday we would have to return to the Council – or the Council would come for us. In the end, Meera was just too important and like it or not, she had been given a gift. Somehow, one way or another, we would return.

But, for now at least… for however brief a time it might turn out to be… we would just run, together… side by side… and see where our legs took us.

The Hirono Chronicles
will return with
Spirit War

Printed in Great Britain
by Amazon